P9-DNC-127

GOSCINNY AND UDERZO
PRESENT
An Asterix Adventure

ASTERIX IN SWITZERLAND

Written by RENÉ GOSCINNY *and Illustrated by* ALBERT UDERZO

Translated by Anthea Bell *and* Derek Hockridge

Asterix titles available now

1 Asterix the Gaul
2 Asterix and the Golden Sickle
3 Asterix and the Goths
4 Asterix the Gladiator
5 Asterix and the Banquet
6 Asterix and Cleopatra
7 Asterix and the Big Fight
8 Asterix in Britain
9 Asterix and the Normans
10 Asterix the Legionary
11 Asterix and the Chieftain's Shield
12 Asterix at the Olympic Games
13 Asterix and the Cauldron
14 Asterix in Spain
15 Asterixand the Roman Agent
16 Asterix in Switzerland
17 The Mansions of the Gods
18 Asterix and the Laurel Wreath
19 Asterix and the Soothsayer
20 Asterix in Corsica
21 Asterix and Caesar's Gift
22 Asterix and the Great Crossing
23 Obelix and Co.
24 Asterix in Belgium
25 Asterix and the Great Divide
26 Asterix and the Black Gold
27 Asterix and Son
28 Asterix and the Magic Carpet
29 Asterix and the Secret Weapon
30 Asterix and Obelix All at Sea
31 Asterix and the Actress
32 Asterix and the Class Act
33 Asterix and the Falling Sky

Coming soon

Asterix versus Caesar
The Twelve Tasks of Asterix
Asterix Conquers America
Operation Getafix

Original title: *Astérix chez les Helvètes*

5 7 9 10 8 6

Exclusive licensee: Orion Publishing Group
Translators: Anthea Bell and Derek Hockridge
Typography: Bryony Newhouse

This revised edition first published in 2004 by Orion Books Ltd,
Orion House, 5 Upper Saint Martin's Lane, London WC2H 9EA

Printed in France by Qualibris

http://gb.asterix.com
www.orionbooks.co.uk

A CIP record for this book is available from the British Library

ISBN-13 978 0 75286 634 5 (cased)
ISBN-13 978 0 75286 635 2 (paperback)

Distributed in the United States of America by Sterling Publishing Co. Inc.
387 Park Avenue South, New York, NY 10016

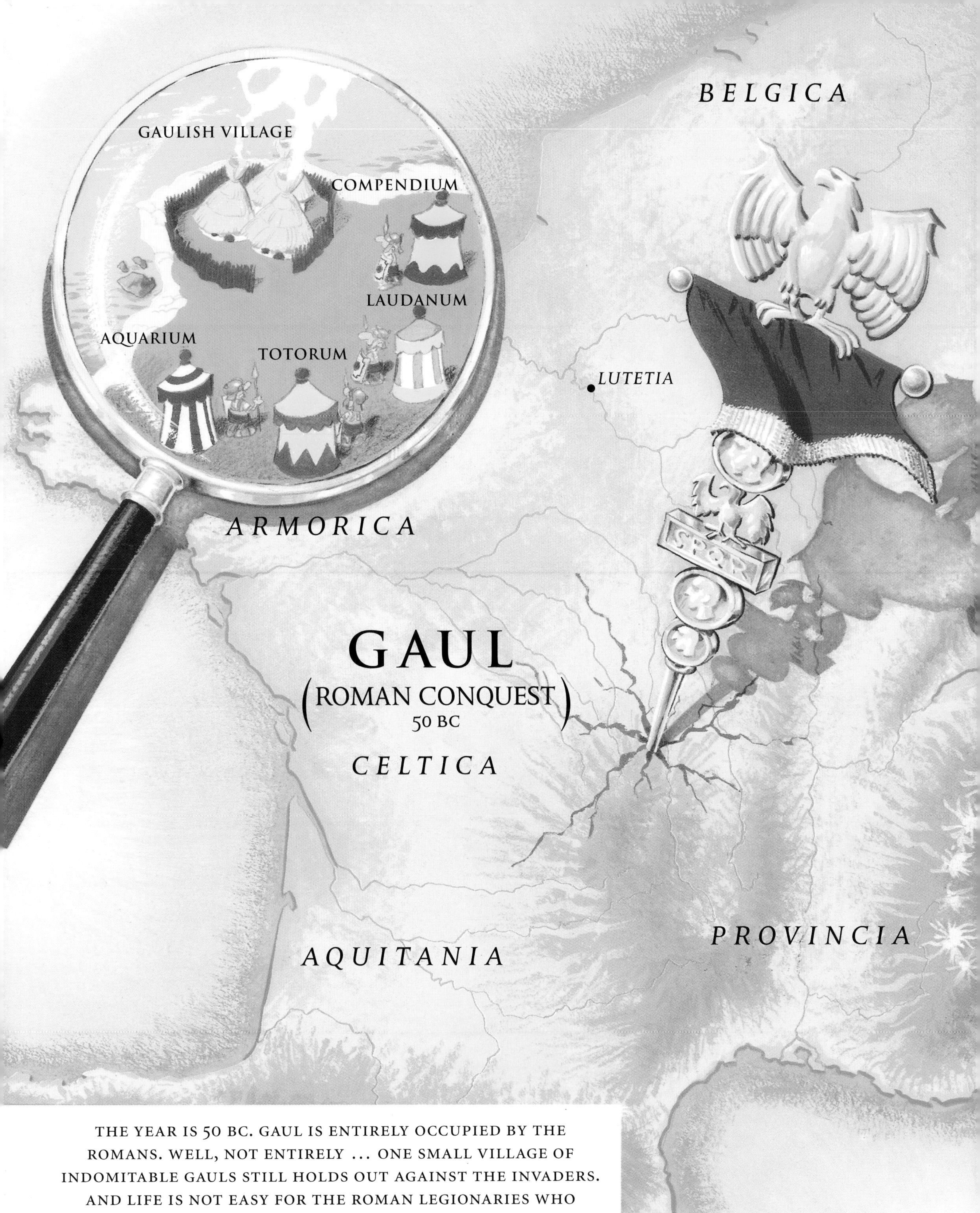
BELGICA
GAULISH VILLAGE
COMPENDIUM
LAUDANUM
AQUARIUM
TOTORUM
LUTETIA
SPQR
ARMORICA
GAUL
(ROMAN CONQUEST)
50 BC
CELTICA
PROVINCIA
AQUITANIA

THE YEAR IS 50 BC. GAUL IS ENTIRELY OCCUPIED BY THE ROMANS. WELL, NOT ENTIRELY ... ONE SMALL VILLAGE OF INDOMITABLE GAULS STILL HOLDS OUT AGAINST THE INVADERS. AND LIFE IS NOT EASY FOR THE ROMAN LEGIONARIES WHO GARRISON THE FORTIFIED CAMPS OF TOTORUM, AQUARIUM, LAUDANUM AND COMPENDIUM ...

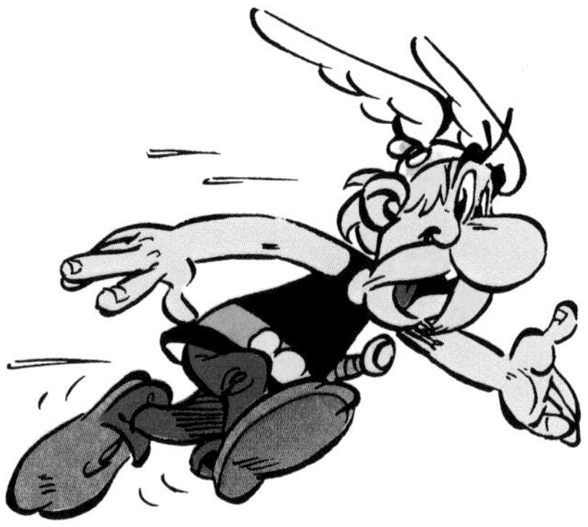

ASTERIX, THE HERO OF THESE ADVENTURES. A SHREWD, CUNNING LITTLE WARRIOR, ALL PERILOUS MISSIONS ARE IMMEDIATELY ENTRUSTED TO HIM. ASTERIX GETS HIS SUPERHUMAN STRENGTH FROM THE MAGIC POTION BREWED BY THE DRUID GETAFIX . . .

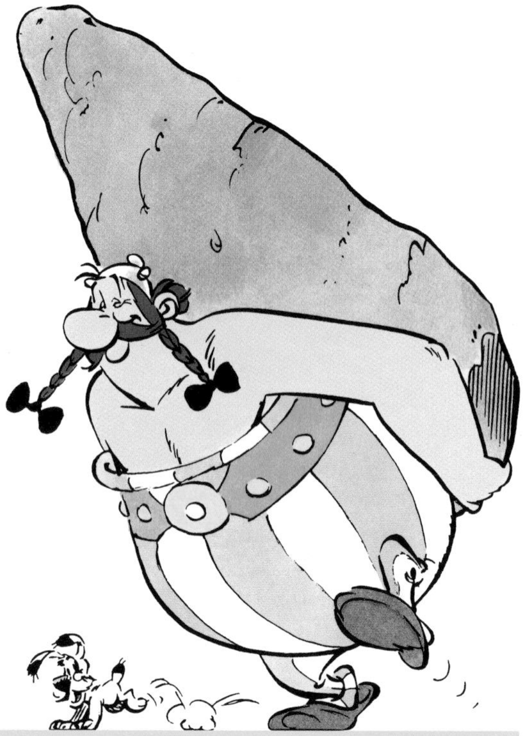

OBELIX, ASTERIX'S INSEPARABLE FRIEND. A MENHIR DELIVERY MAN BY TRADE, ADDICTED TO WILD BOAR. OBELIX IS ALWAYS READY TO DROP EVERYTHING AND GO OFF ON A NEW ADVENTURE WITH ASTERIX – SO LONG AS THERE'S WILD BOAR TO EAT, AND PLENTY OF FIGHTING. HIS CONSTANT COMPANION IS DOGMATIX, THE ONLY KNOWN CANINE ECOLOGIST, WHO HOWLS WITH DESPAIR WHEN A TREE IS CUT DOWN.

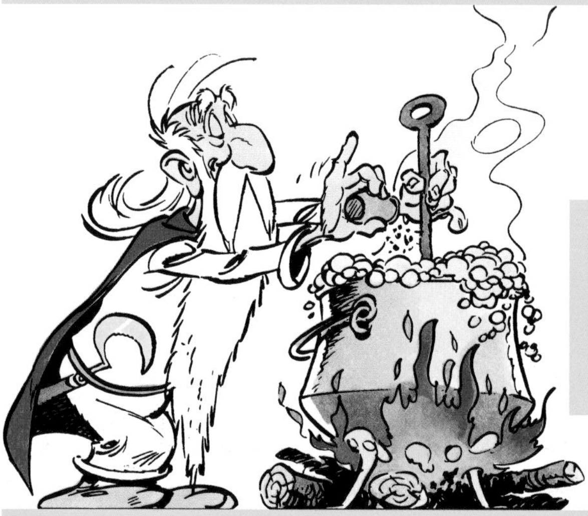

GETAFIX, THE VENERABLE VILLAGE DRUID, GATHERS MISTLETOE AND BREWS MAGIC POTIONS. HIS SPECIALITY IS THE POTION WHICH GIVES THE DRINKER SUPERHUMAN STRENGTH. BUT GETAFIX ALSO HAS OTHER RECIPES UP HIS SLEEVE . . .

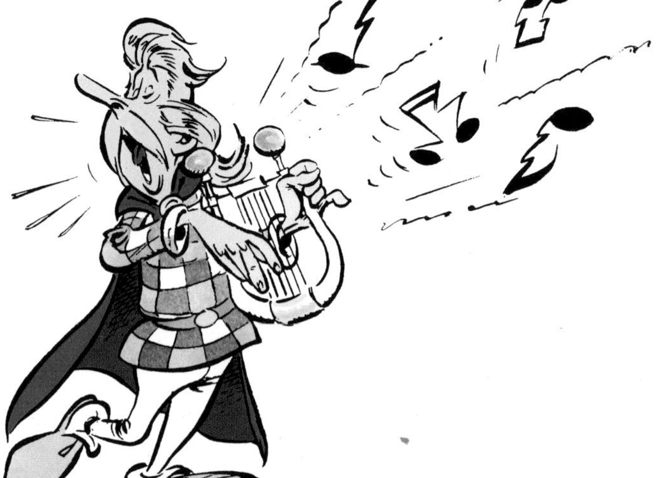

CACOFONIX, THE BARD. OPINION IS DIVIDED AS TO HIS MUSICAL GIFTS. CACOFONIX THINKS HE'S A GENIUS. EVERYONE ELSE THINKS HE'S UNSPEAKABLE. BUT SO LONG AS HE DOESN'T SPEAK, LET ALONE SING, EVERYBODY LIKES HIM . . .

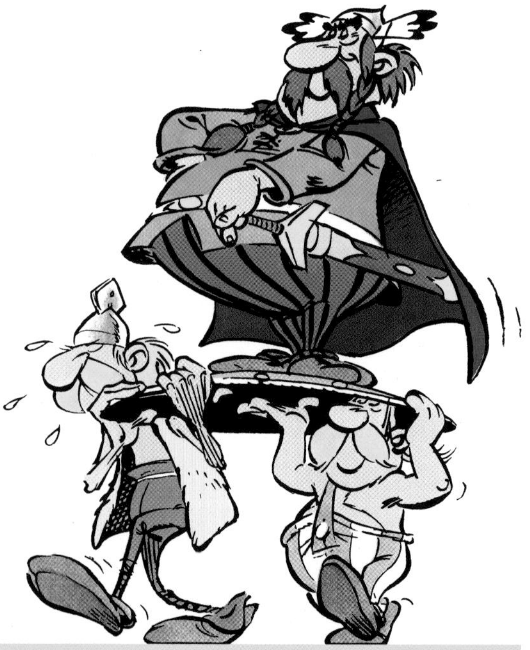

FINALLY, VITALSTATISTIX, THE CHIEF OF THE TRIBE. MAJESTIC, BRAVE AND HOT-TEMPERED, THE OLD WARRIOR IS RESPECTED BY HIS MEN AND FEARED BY HIS ENEMIES. VITALSTATISTIX HIMSELF HAS ONLY ONE FEAR, HE IS AFRAID THE SKY MAY FALL ON HIS HEAD TOMORROW. BUT AS HE ALWAYS SAYS, TOMORROW NEVER COMES.

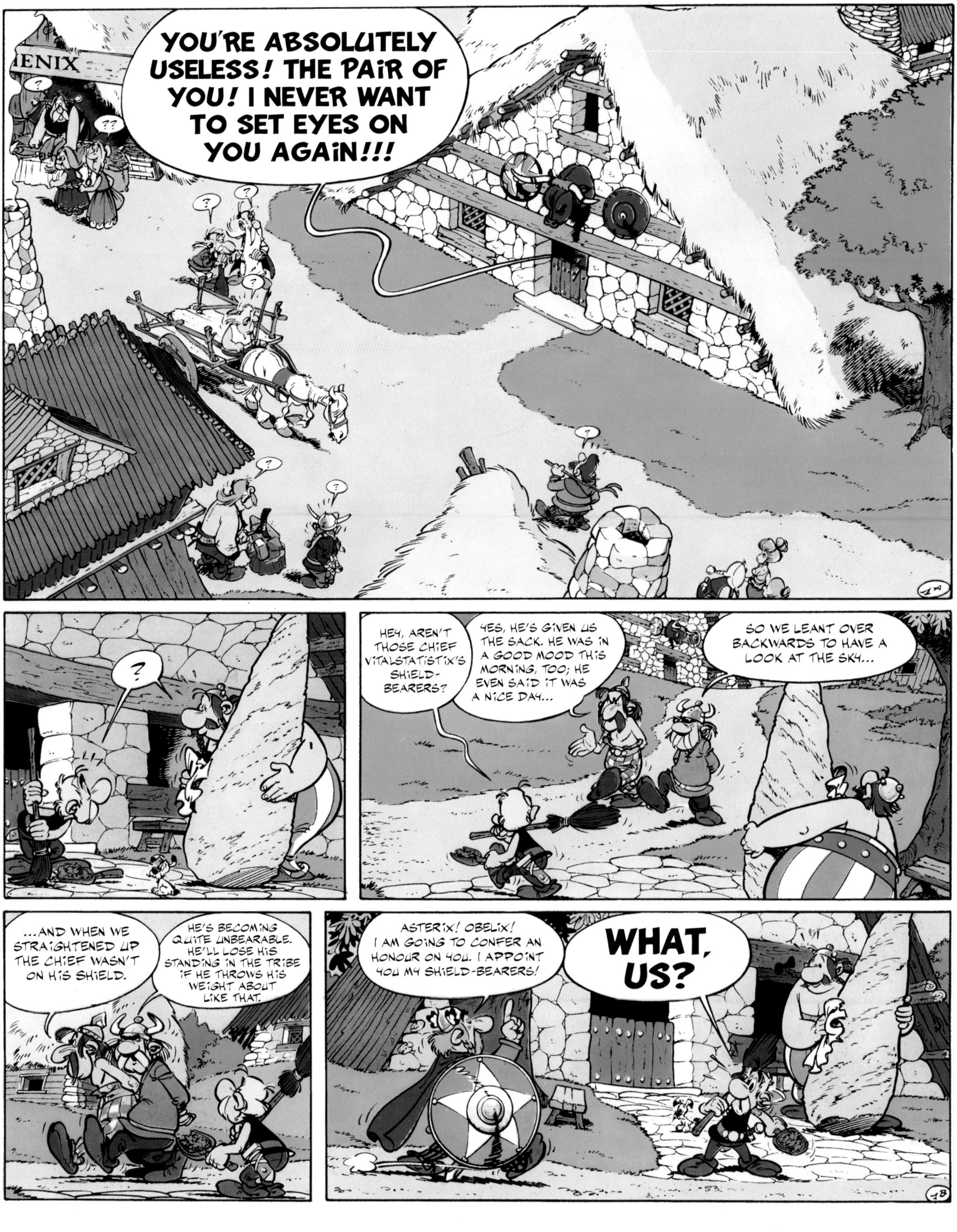
YOU'RE ABSOLUTELY USELESS! THE PAIR OF YOU! I NEVER WANT TO SET EYES ON YOU AGAIN!!!
?
HEY, AREN'T THOSE CHIEF VITALSTATISTIX'S SHIELD-BEARERS?
YES, HE'S GIVEN US THE SACK. HE WAS IN A GOOD MOOD THIS MORNING, TOO; HE EVEN SAID IT WAS A NICE DAY...
SO WE LEANT OVER BACKWARDS TO HAVE A LOOK AT THE SKY...
...AND WHEN WE STRAIGHTENED UP THE CHIEF WASN'T ON HIS SHIELD.
HE'S BECOMING QUITE UNBEARABLE. HE'LL LOSE HIS STANDING IN THE TRIBE IF HE THROWS HIS WEIGHT ABOUT LIKE THAT.
ASTERIX! OBELIX! I AM GOING TO CONFER AN HONOUR ON YOU. I APPOINT YOU MY SHIELD-BEARERS!
WHAT, US?

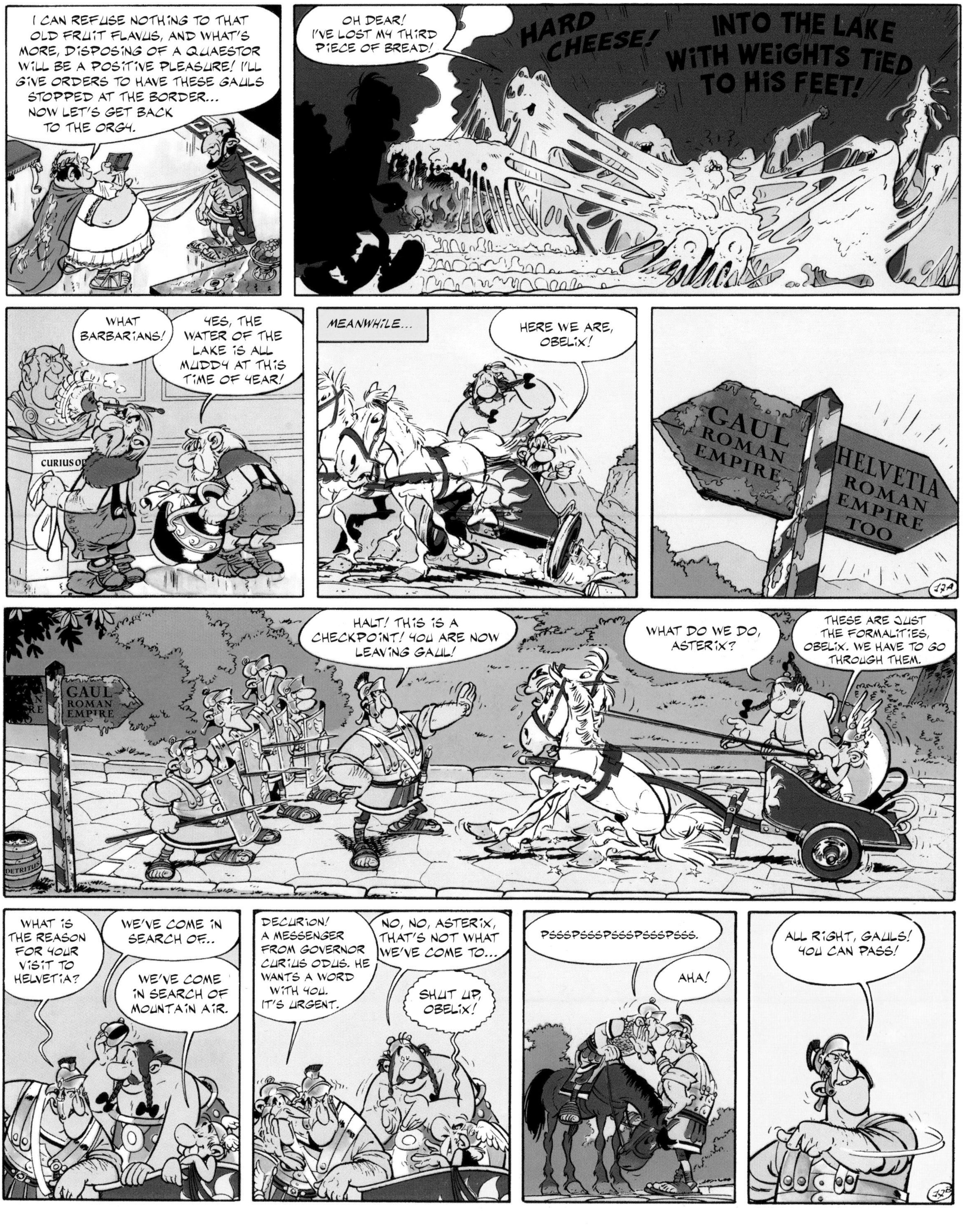
I CAN REFUSE NOTHING TO THAT OLD FRUIT FLAVUS, AND WHAT'S MORE, DISPOSING OF A QUAESTOR WILL BE A POSITIVE PLEASURE! I'LL GIVE ORDERS TO HAVE THESE GAULS STOPPED AT THE BORDER... NOW LET'S GET BACK TO THE ORGY.
OH DEAR! I'VE LOST MY THIRD PIECE OF BREAD!
HARD CHEESE!
INTO THE LAKE WITH WEIGHTS TIED TO HIS FEET!
WHAT BARBARIANS!
YES, THE WATER OF THE LAKE IS ALL MUDDY AT THIS TIME OF YEAR!
CURIUSOD
MEANWHILE...
HERE WE ARE, OBELIX!
GAUL ROMAN EMPIRE
HELVETIA ROMAN EMPIRE TOO
HALT! THIS IS A CHECKPOINT! YOU ARE NOW LEAVING GAUL!
GAUL ROMAN EMPIRE
DETRITUS
WHAT DO WE DO, ASTERIX?
THESE ARE JUST THE FORMALITIES, OBELIX. WE HAVE TO GO THROUGH THEM.
WHAT IS THE REASON FOR YOUR VISIT TO HELVETIA?
WE'VE COME IN SEARCH OF...
WE'VE COME IN SEARCH OF MOUNTAIN AIR.
DECURION! A MESSENGER FROM GOVERNOR CURIUS ODUS. HE WANTS A WORD WITH YOU. IT'S URGENT.
NO, NO, ASTERIX, THAT'S NOT WHAT WE'VE COME TO...
SHUT UP, OBELIX!
PSSSPSSSPSSSPSSSPSSS.
AHA!
ALL RIGHT, GAULS! YOU CAN PASS!

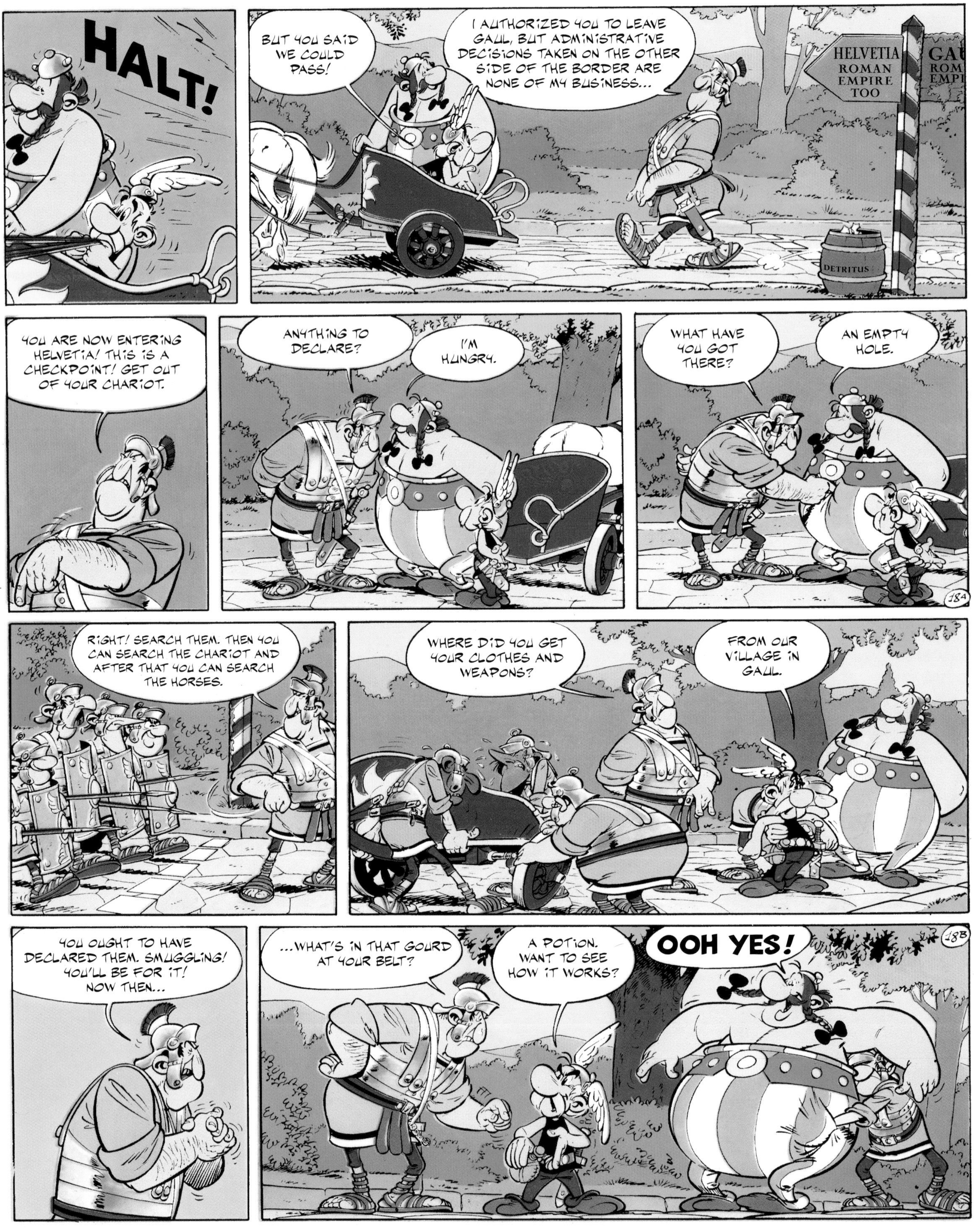
HALT!
BUT YOU SAID WE COULD PASS!
I AUTHORIZED YOU TO LEAVE GAUL, BUT ADMINISTRATIVE DECISIONS TAKEN ON THE OTHER SIDE OF THE BORDER ARE NONE OF MY BUSINESS...
HELVETIA ROMAN EMPIRE TOO
GAU ROM EMPI
DETRITUS
YOU ARE NOW ENTERING HELVETIA! THIS IS A CHECKPOINT! GET OUT OF YOUR CHARIOT.
ANYTHING TO DECLARE?
I'M HUNGRY.
WHAT HAVE YOU GOT THERE?
AN EMPTY HOLE.
18A
RIGHT! SEARCH THEM. THEN YOU CAN SEARCH THE CHARIOT AND AFTER THAT YOU CAN SEARCH THE HORSES.
WHERE DID YOU GET YOUR CLOTHES AND WEAPONS?
FROM OUR VILLAGE IN GAUL.
YOU OUGHT TO HAVE DECLARED THEM. SMUGGLING! YOU'LL BE FOR IT! NOW THEN...
...WHAT'S IN THAT GOURD AT YOUR BELT?
A POTION. WANT TO SEE HOW IT WORKS?
OOH YES!
18B

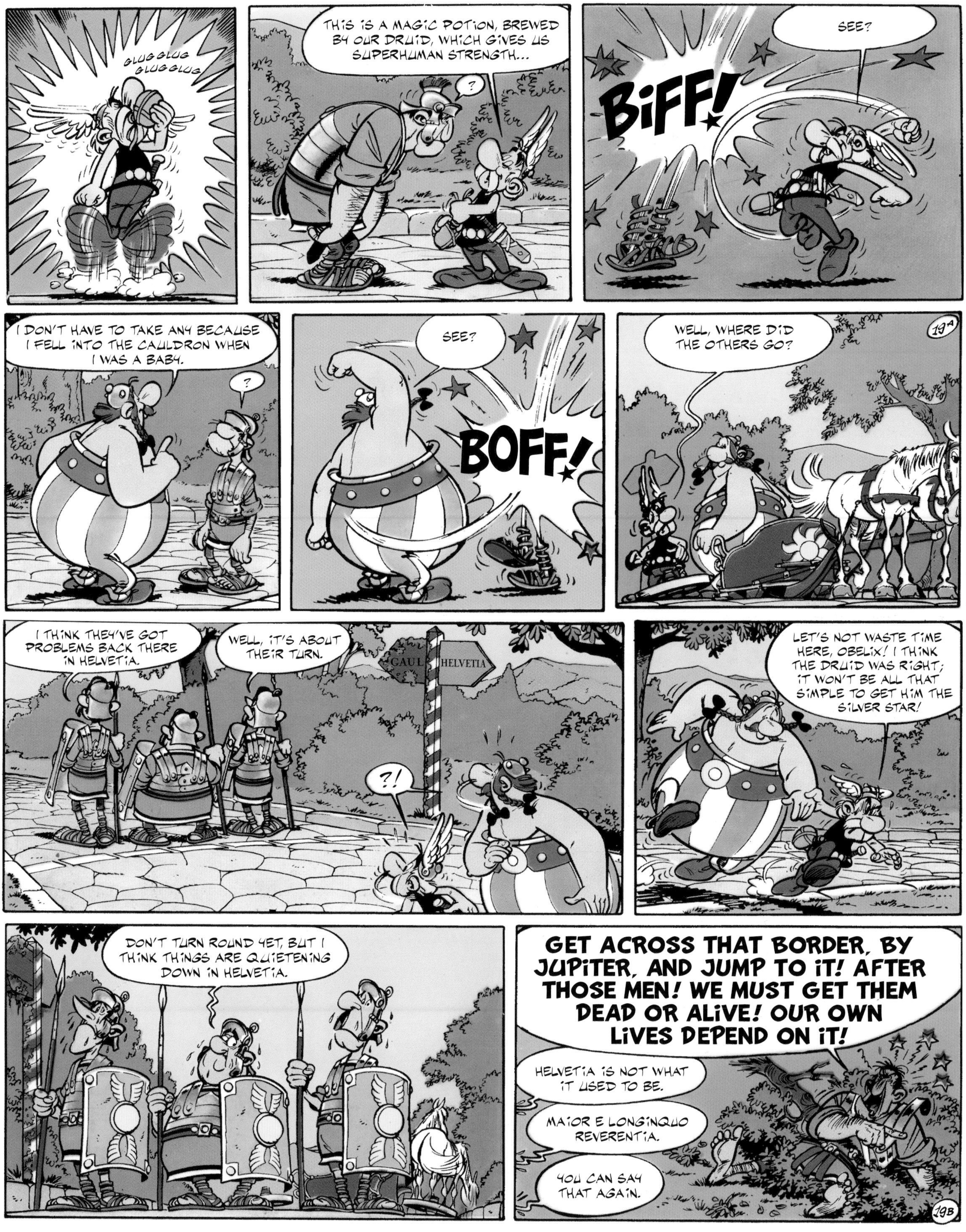
GLUG GLUG GLUG GLUG
THIS IS A MAGIC POTION, BREWED BY OUR DRUID, WHICH GIVES US SUPERHUMAN STRENGTH...
?
SEE?
BIFF!
I DON'T HAVE TO TAKE ANY BECAUSE I FELL INTO THE CAULDRON WHEN I WAS A BABY.
?
SEE?
BOFF!
WELL, WHERE DID THE OTHERS GO?
19A
I THINK THEY'VE GOT PROBLEMS BACK THERE IN HELVETIA.
WELL, IT'S ABOUT THEIR TURN.
GAUL
HELVETIA
?!
LET'S NOT WASTE TIME HERE, OBELIX! I THINK THE DRUID WAS RIGHT; IT WON'T BE ALL THAT SIMPLE TO GET HIM THE SILVER STAR!
DON'T TURN ROUND YET, BUT I THINK THINGS ARE QUIETENING DOWN IN HELVETIA.
GET ACROSS THAT BORDER, BY JUPITER, AND JUMP TO IT! AFTER THOSE MEN! WE MUST GET THEM DEAD OR ALIVE! OUR OWN LIVES DEPEND ON IT!
HELVETIA IS NOT WHAT IT USED TO BE.
MAIOR E LONGINQUO REVERENTIA.
YOU CAN SAY THAT AGAIN.
19B

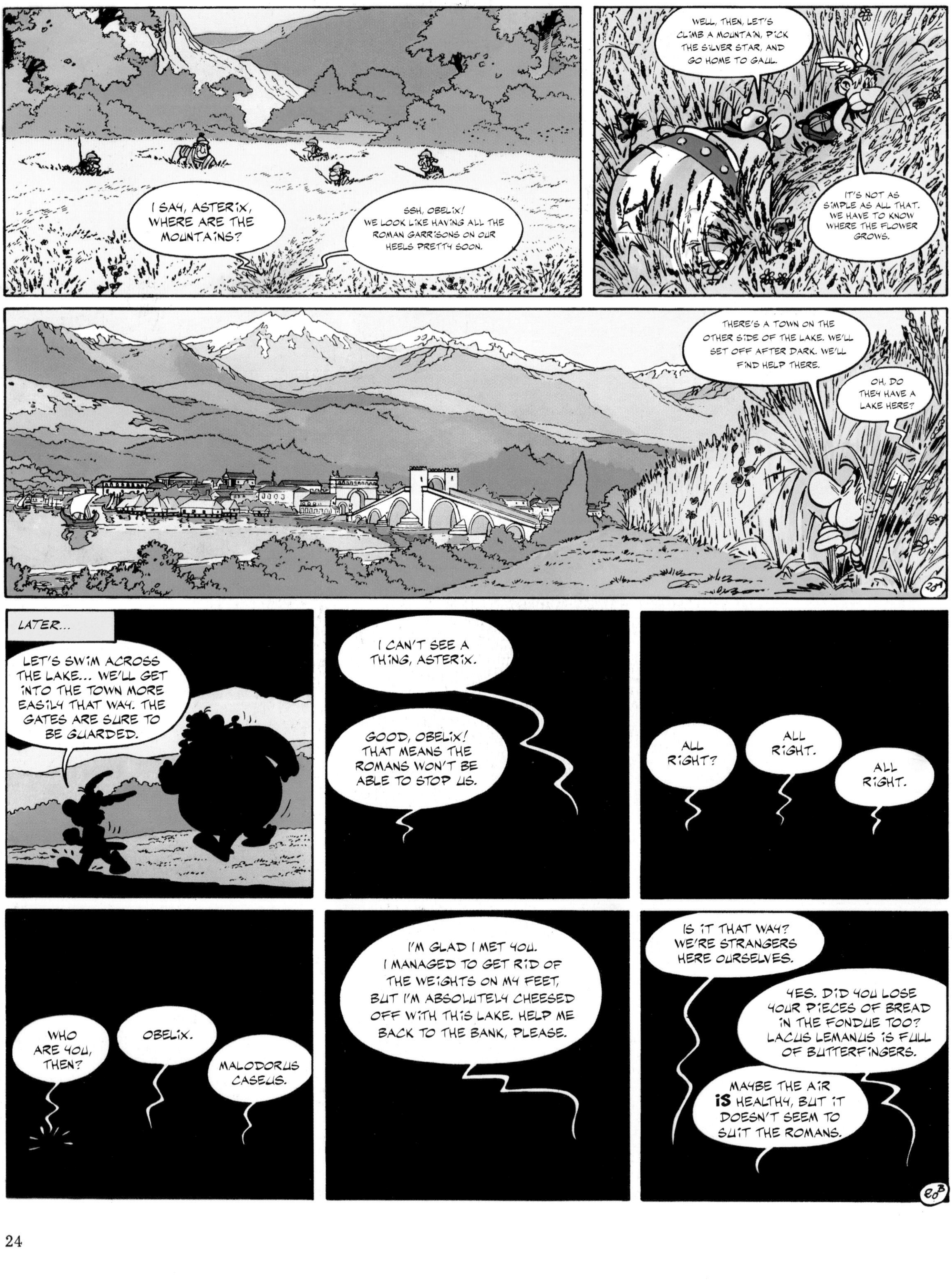
I SAY, ASTERIX, WHERE ARE THE MOUNTAINS?
SSH, OBELIX! WE LOOK LIKE HAVING ALL THE ROMAN GARRISONS ON OUR HEELS PRETTY SOON.
WELL, THEN, LET'S CLIMB A MOUNTAIN, PICK THE SILVER STAR, AND GO HOME TO GAUL.
IT'S NOT AS SIMPLE AS ALL THAT. WE HAVE TO KNOW WHERE THE FLOWER GROWS.
THERE'S A TOWN ON THE OTHER SIDE OF THE LAKE. WE'LL SET OFF AFTER DARK. WE'LL FIND HELP THERE.
OH, DO THEY HAVE A LAKE HERE?
LATER...
LET'S SWIM ACROSS THE LAKE... WE'LL GET INTO THE TOWN MORE EASILY THAT WAY. THE GATES ARE SURE TO BE GUARDED.
I CAN'T SEE A THING, ASTERIX.
GOOD, OBELIX! THAT MEANS THE ROMANS WON'T BE ABLE TO STOP US.
ALL RIGHT?
ALL RIGHT.
ALL RIGHT.
WHO ARE YOU, THEN?
OBELIX.
MALODORUS CASEUS.
I'M GLAD I MET YOU. I MANAGED TO GET RID OF THE WEIGHTS ON MY FEET, BUT I'M ABSOLUTELY CHEESED OFF WITH THIS LAKE. HELP ME BACK TO THE BANK, PLEASE.
IS IT THAT WAY? WE'RE STRANGERS HERE OURSELVES.
YES. DID YOU LOSE YOUR PIECES OF BREAD IN THE FONDUE TOO? LACUS LEMANUS IS FULL OF BUTTERFINGERS.
MAYBE THE AIR IS HEALTHY, BUT IT DOESN'T SEEM TO SUIT THE ROMANS.

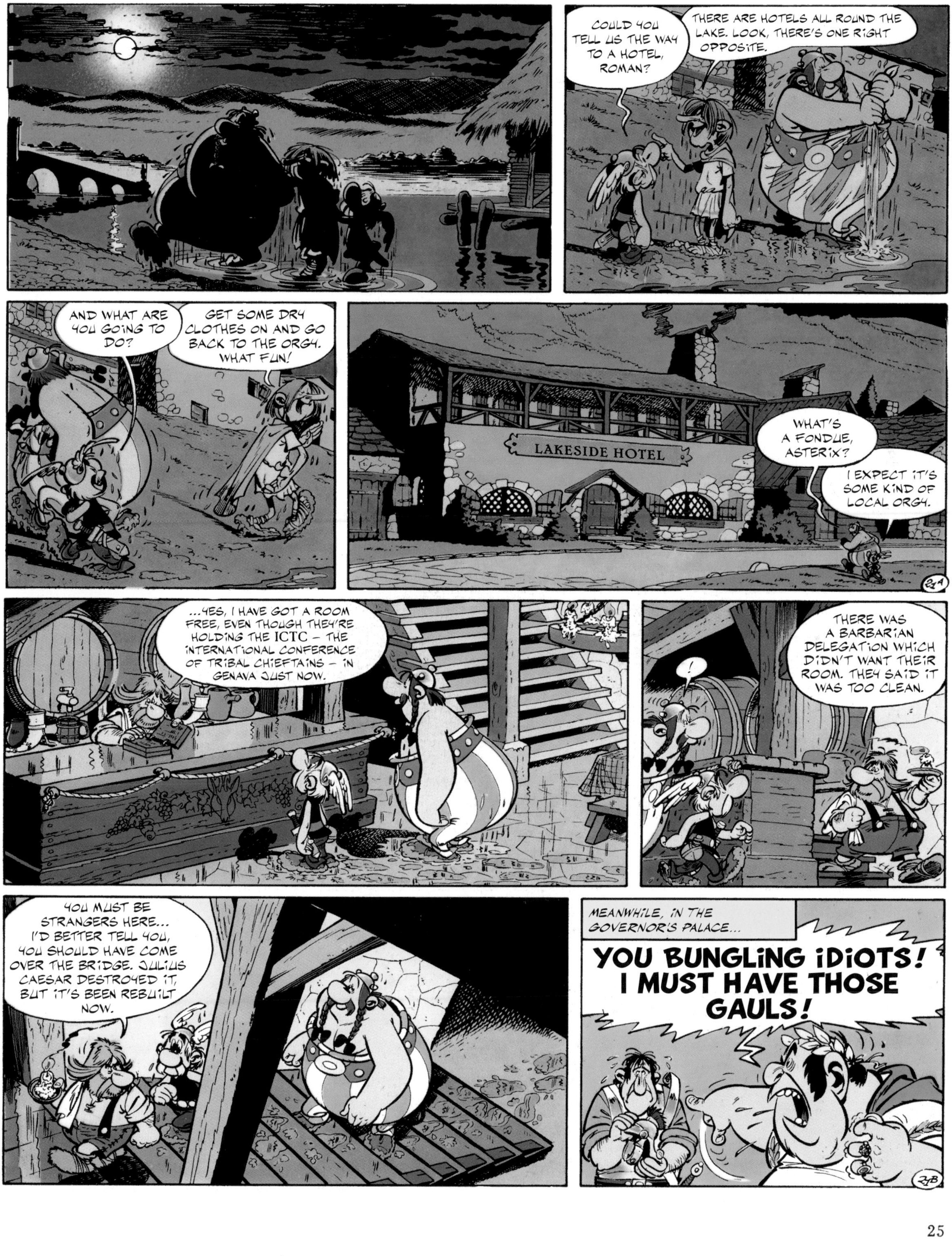
COULD YOU TELL US THE WAY TO A HOTEL, ROMAN?
THERE ARE HOTELS ALL ROUND THE LAKE. LOOK, THERE'S ONE RIGHT OPPOSITE.
AND WHAT ARE YOU GOING TO DO?
GET SOME DRY CLOTHES ON AND GO BACK TO THE ORGY. WHAT FUN!
LAKESIDE HOTEL
WHAT'S A FONDUE, ASTERIX?
I EXPECT IT'S SOME KIND OF LOCAL ORGY.
...YES, I HAVE GOT A ROOM FREE, EVEN THOUGH THEY'RE HOLDING THE ICTC – THE INTERNATIONAL CONFERENCE OF TRIBAL CHIEFTAINS – IN GENAVA JUST NOW.
!
THERE WAS A BARBARIAN DELEGATION WHICH DIDN'T WANT THEIR ROOM. THEY SAID IT WAS TOO CLEAN.
YOU MUST BE STRANGERS HERE... I'D BETTER TELL YOU, YOU SHOULD HAVE COME OVER THE BRIDGE. JULIUS CAESAR DESTROYED IT, BUT IT'S BEEN REBUILT NOW.
MEANWHILE, IN THE GOVERNOR'S PALACE...
YOU BUNGLING IDIOTS! I MUST HAVE THOSE GAULS!

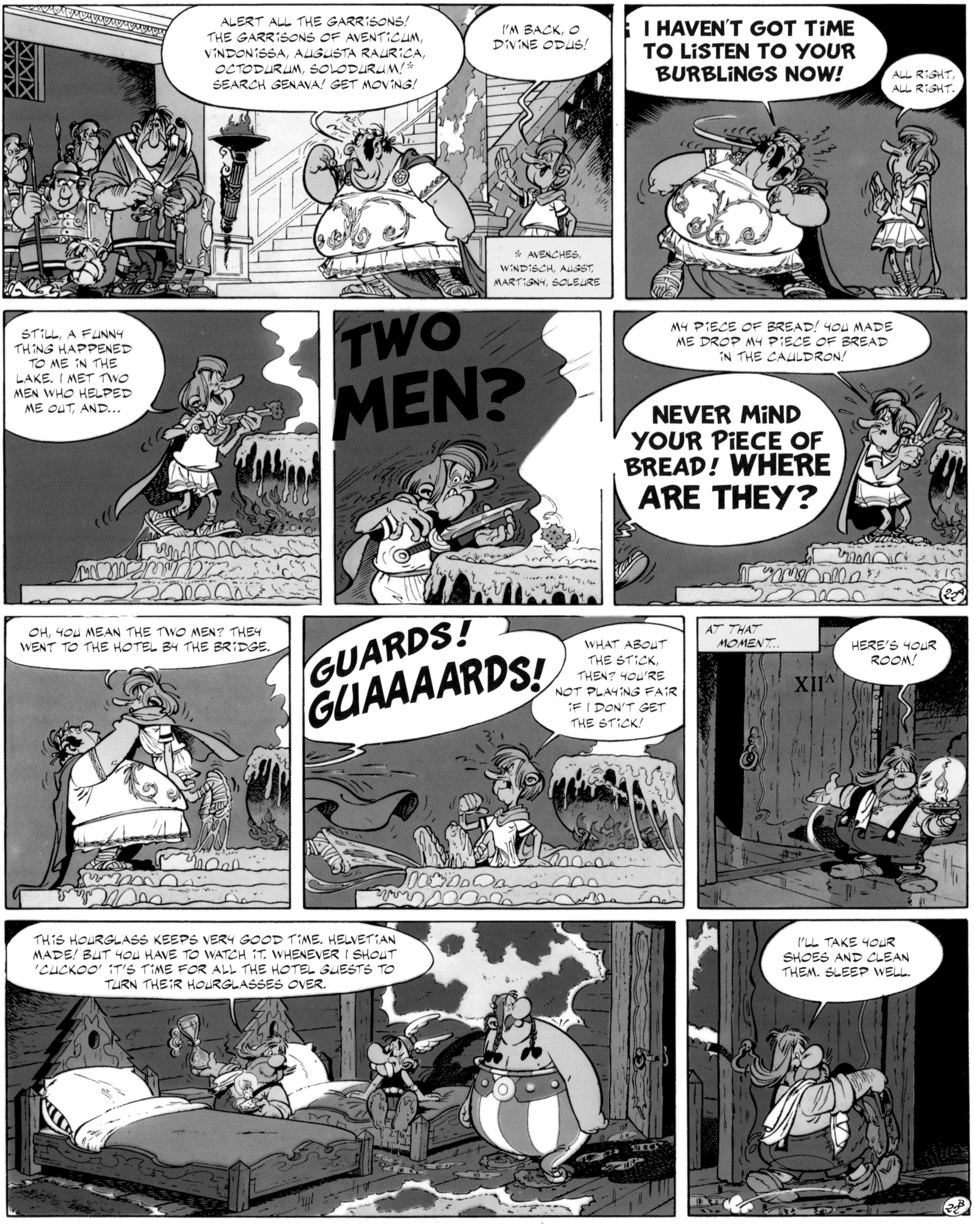
ALERT ALL THE GARRISONS! THE GARRISONS OF AVENTICUM, VINDONISSA, AUGUSTA RAURICA, OCTODURUM, SOLODURUM!* SEARCH GENAVA! GET MOVING!
I'M BACK, O DIVINE ODUS!
* AVENCHES, WINDISCH, AUGST, MARTIGNY, SOLEURE
I HAVEN'T GOT TIME TO LISTEN TO YOUR BURBLINGS NOW!
ALL RIGHT, ALL RIGHT.
STILL, A FUNNY THING HAPPENED TO ME IN THE LAKE. I MET TWO MEN WHO HELPED ME OUT, AND...
TWO MEN?
MY PIECE OF BREAD! YOU MADE ME DROP MY PIECE OF BREAD IN THE CAULDRON!
NEVER MIND YOUR PIECE OF BREAD! WHERE ARE THEY?
OH, YOU MEAN THE TWO MEN? THEY WENT TO THE HOTEL BY THE BRIDGE.
GUARDS! GUAAAARDS!
WHAT ABOUT THE STICK, THEN? YOU'RE NOT PLAYING FAIR IF I DON'T GET THE STICK!
AT THAT MOMENT...
XII^A
HERE'S YOUR ROOM!
THIS HOURGLASS KEEPS VERY GOOD TIME. HELVETIAN MADE! BUT YOU HAVE TO WATCH IT. WHENEVER I SHOUT 'CUCKOO' IT'S TIME FOR ALL THE HOTEL GUESTS TO TURN THEIR HOURGLASSES OVER.
I'LL TAKE YOUR SHOES AND CLEAN THEM. SLEEP WELL.

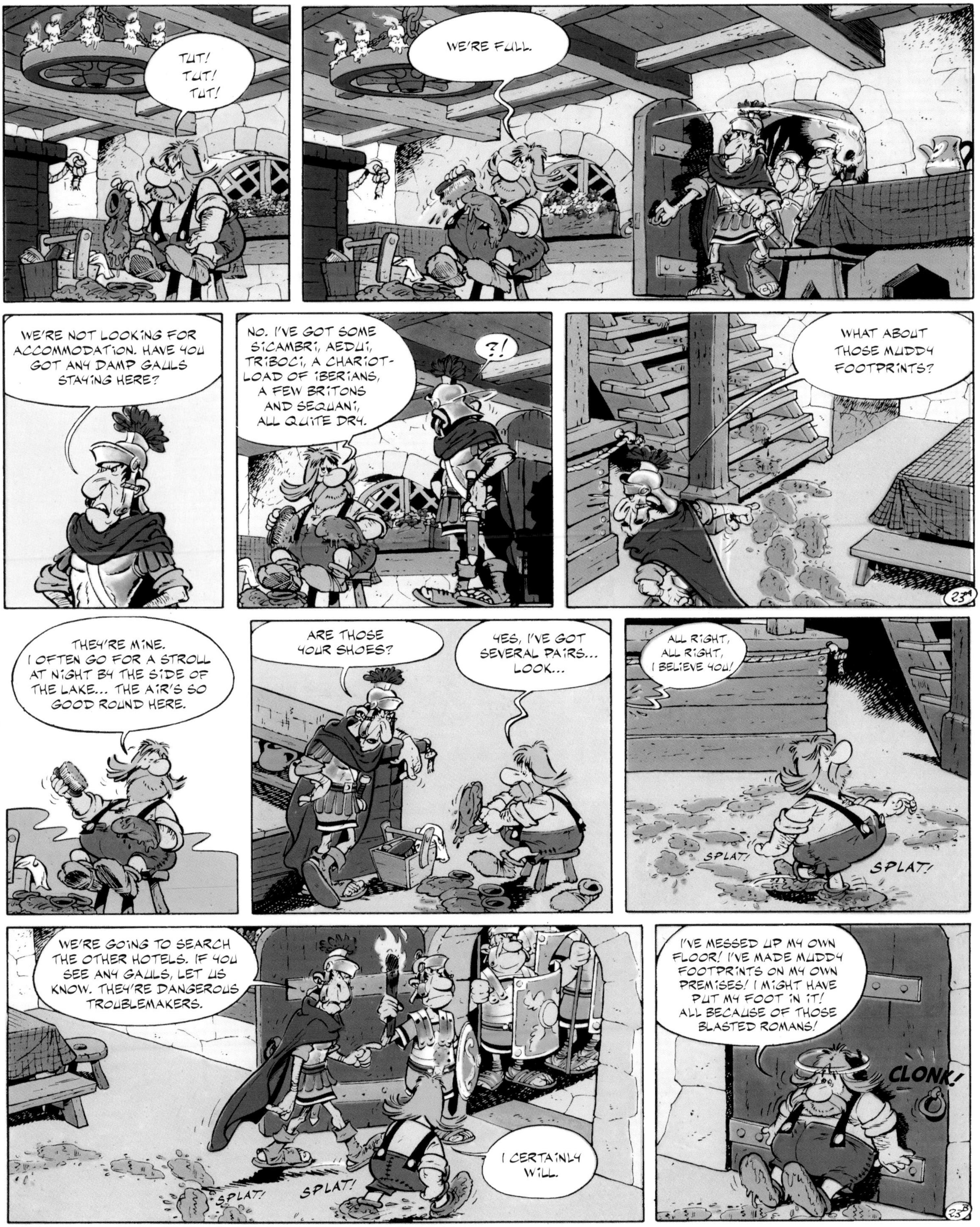
TUT! TUT! TUT!
WE'RE FULL.
WE'RE NOT LOOKING FOR ACCOMMODATION. HAVE YOU GOT ANY DAMP GAULS STAYING HERE?
NO. I'VE GOT SOME SICAMBRI, AEDUI, TRIBOCI, A CHARIOT-LOAD OF IBERIANS, A FEW BRITONS AND SEQUANI, ALL QUITE DRY.
?!
WHAT ABOUT THOSE MUDDY FOOTPRINTS?
THEY'RE MINE. I OFTEN GO FOR A STROLL AT NIGHT BY THE SIDE OF THE LAKE... THE AIR'S SO GOOD ROUND HERE.
ARE THOSE YOUR SHOES?
YES, I'VE GOT SEVERAL PAIRS... LOOK...
ALL RIGHT, ALL RIGHT, I BELIEVE YOU!
SPLAT!
SPLAT!
WE'RE GOING TO SEARCH THE OTHER HOTELS. IF YOU SEE ANY GAULS, LET US KNOW. THEY'RE DANGEROUS TROUBLEMAKERS.
I CERTAINLY WILL.
SPLAT!
SPLAT!
I'VE MESSED UP MY OWN FLOOR! I'VE MADE MUDDY FOOTPRINTS ON MY OWN PREMISES! I MIGHT HAVE PUT MY FOOT IN IT! ALL BECAUSE OF THOSE BLASTED ROMANS!
CLONK!

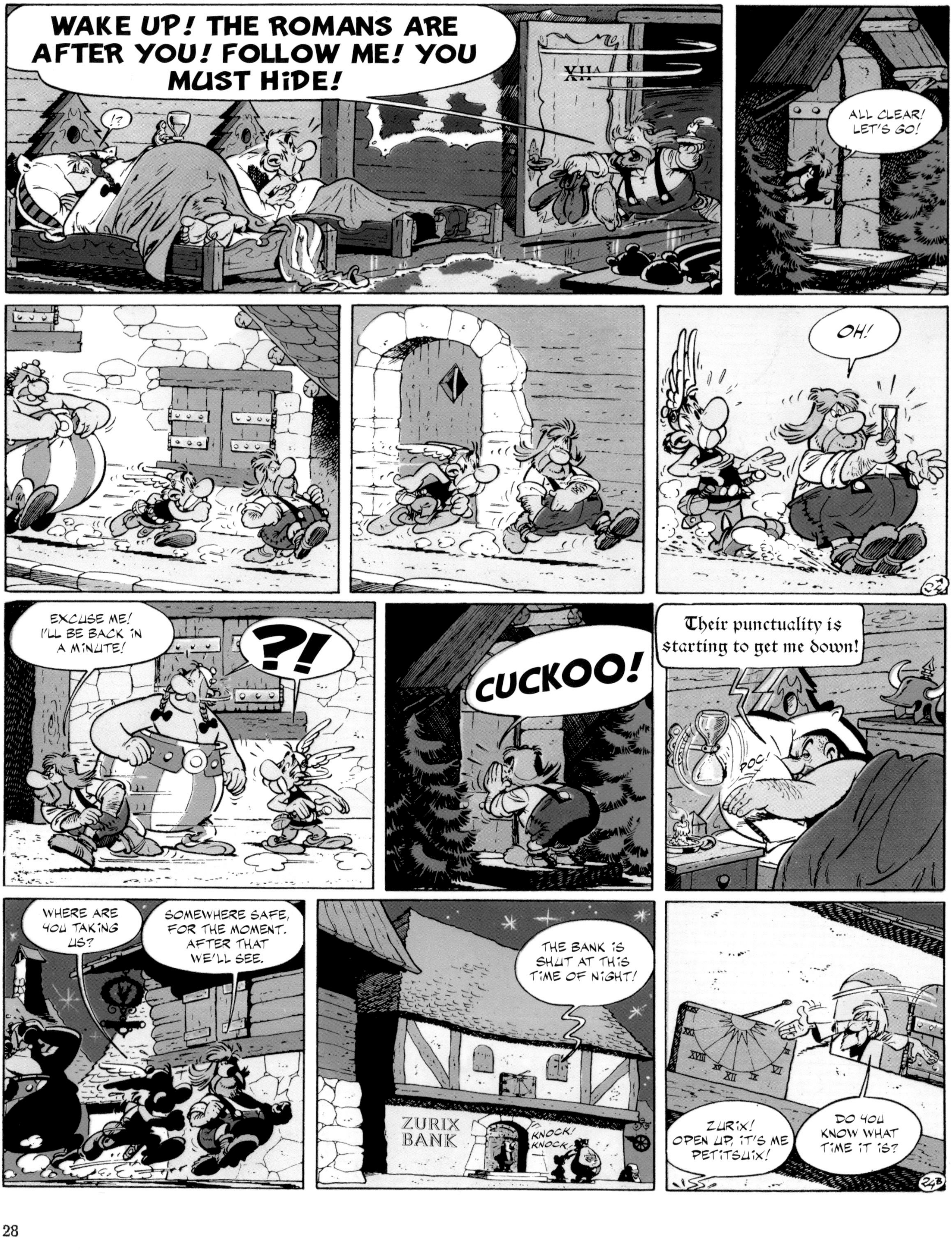
WAKE UP! THE ROMANS ARE AFTER YOU! FOLLOW ME! YOU MUST HIDE!
!?
XII
ALL CLEAR! LET'S GO!
OH!
EXCUSE ME! I'LL BE BACK IN A MINUTE!
?!
CUCKOO!
Their punctuality is starting to get me down!
POC!
WHERE ARE YOU TAKING US?
SOMEWHERE SAFE, FOR THE MOMENT. AFTER THAT WE'LL SEE.
THE BANK IS SHUT AT THIS TIME OF NIGHT!
ZURIX BANK
KNOCK! KNOCK!
ZURIX! OPEN UP, IT'S ME PETITSUIX!
DO YOU KNOW WHAT TIME IT IS?

THE ROMANS ARE AFTER THESE TWO MEN. THEY'RE SEARCHING THE WHOLE TOWN. WE MUST SAVE THEM!

YES, OF COURSE. YOU HAVE OUR SYMPATHY. WE HAVE OFTEN FOUGHT AGAINST THE ROMANS, AND JULIUS CAESAR CONSIDERS US FORMIDABLE ENEMIES... BUT WHERE CAN WE HIDE YOU?

I HAD THOUGHT OF ONE OF YOUR SAFES, IN THE VAULT...

YOU'D HAVE TO OPEN AN ACCOUNT.

WHAT, TO HIDE IN A SAFE?

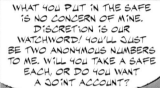

WHAT YOU PUT IN THE SAFE IS NO CONCERN OF MINE. DISCRETION IS OUR WATCHWORD! YOU'LL JUST BE TWO ANONYMOUS NUMBERS TO ME. WILL YOU TAKE A SAFE EACH, OR DO YOU WANT A JOINT ACCOUNT?

IF YOU HAVE A BIG ENOUGH SAFE, WE'D RATHER BE TOGETHER.

THAT'LL BE QUITE IN ORDER. SIGN, PLEASE. THERE, THERE AND THERE.

THIS WAY, PLEASE.

HERE'S YOUR SAFE.

CREEAK!

I'LL COME BACK TOMORROW. WE'LL KEEP YOU IN TOUCH.

THANKS FOR EVERYTHING, PETITSUIX!

WAIT A MOMENT! THERE ARE NO REGULATIONS COVERING THE OPENING OF A SAFE FROM THE INSIDE. IF YOU WANT PETITSUIX TO COME AND OPEN IT, YOU MUST GIVE HIM A POWER OF ATTORNEY!

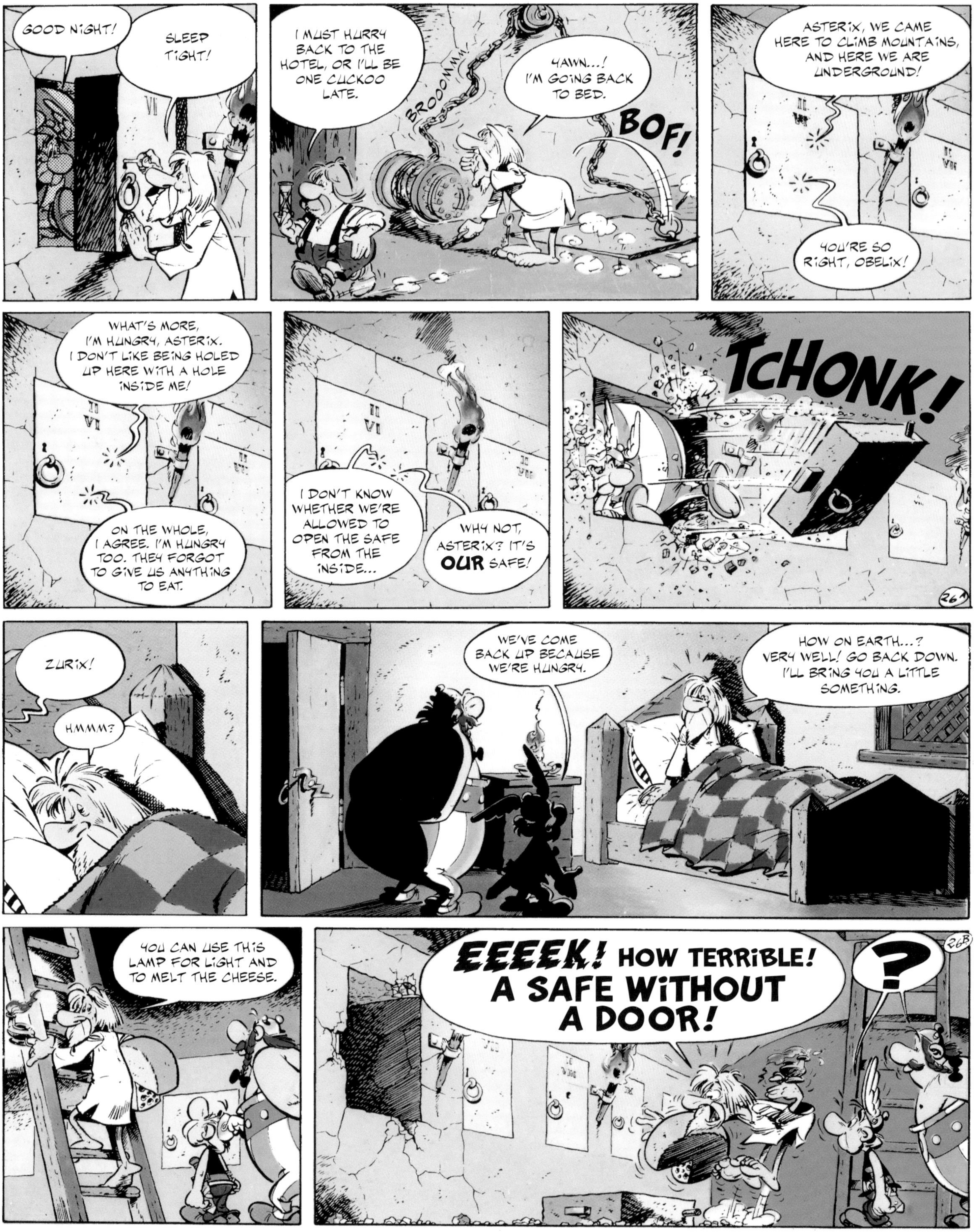
GOOD NIGHT!
SLEEP TIGHT!
I MUST HURRY BACK TO THE HOTEL, OR I'LL BE ONE CUCKOO LATE.
BROOOMM!
YAWN...! I'M GOING BACK TO BED.
BOF!
ASTERIX, WE CAME HERE TO CLIMB MOUNTAINS, AND HERE WE ARE UNDERGROUND!
YOU'RE SO RIGHT, OBELIX!
WHAT'S MORE, I'M HUNGRY, ASTERIX. I DON'T LIKE BEING HOLED UP HERE WITH A HOLE INSIDE ME!
ON THE WHOLE, I AGREE. I'M HUNGRY TOO. THEY FORGOT TO GIVE US ANYTHING TO EAT.
I DON'T KNOW WHETHER WE'RE ALLOWED TO OPEN THE SAFE FROM THE INSIDE...
WHY NOT, ASTERIX? IT'S **OUR** SAFE!
TCHONK!
ZURIX!
HMMM?
WE'VE COME BACK UP BECAUSE WE'RE HUNGRY.
HOW ON EARTH...? VERY WELL! GO BACK DOWN. I'LL BRING YOU A LITTLE SOMETHING.
YOU CAN USE THIS LAMP FOR LIGHT AND TO MELT THE CHEESE.
EEEEK! HOW TERRIBLE! A SAFE WITHOUT A DOOR!
?

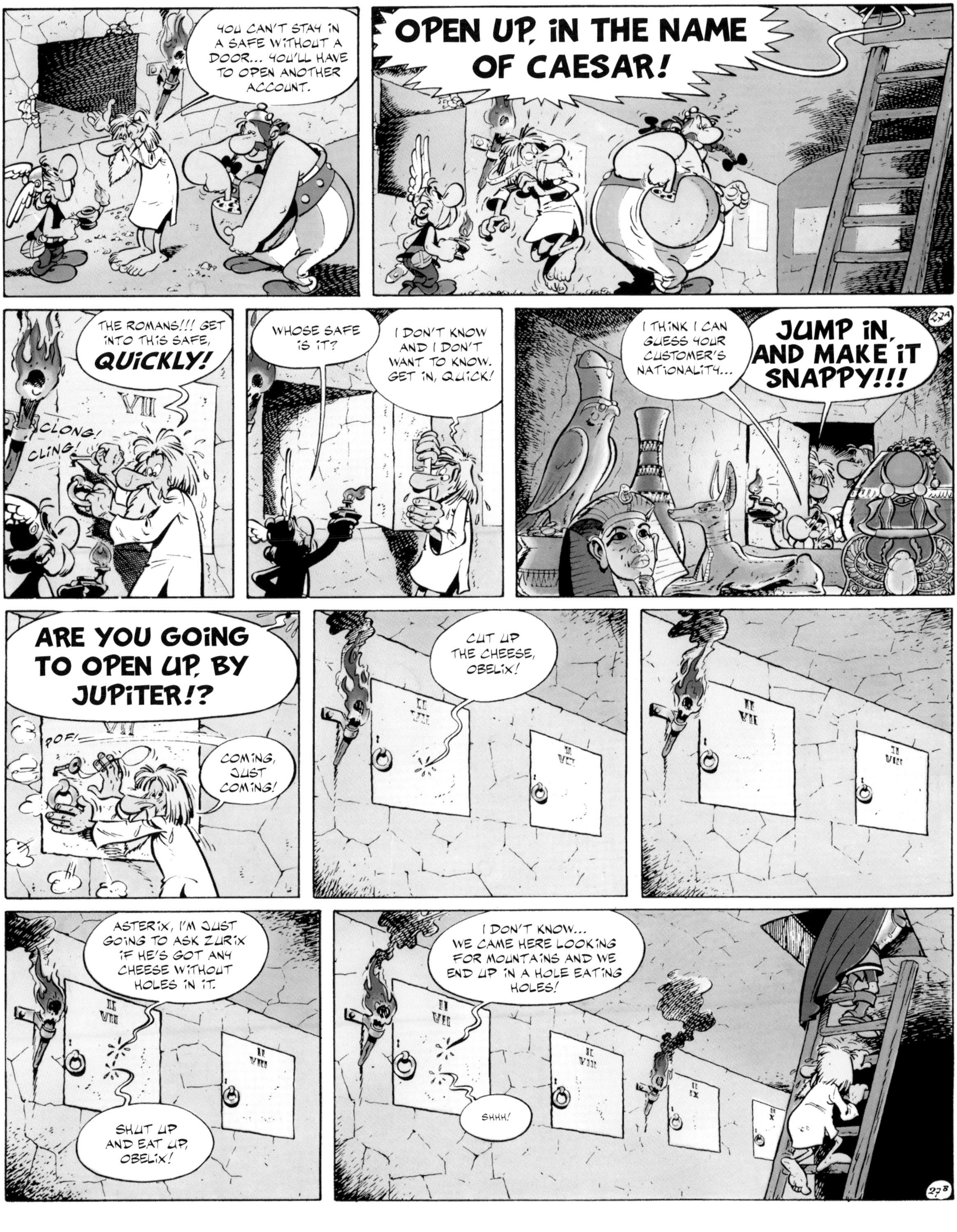
YOU CAN'T STAY IN A SAFE WITHOUT A DOOR... YOU'LL HAVE TO OPEN ANOTHER ACCOUNT.
OPEN UP, IN THE NAME OF CAESAR!
THE ROMANS!!! GET INTO THIS SAFE, QUICKLY!
VII
CLONG! CLING!
WHOSE SAFE IS IT?
I DON'T KNOW AND I DON'T WANT TO KNOW. GET IN, QUICK!
I THINK I CAN GUESS YOUR CUSTOMER'S NATIONALITY...
JUMP IN, AND MAKE IT SNAPPY!!!
27A
ARE YOU GOING TO OPEN UP, BY JUPITER!?
POF!
COMING, JUST COMING!
CUT UP THE CHEESE, OBELIX!
ASTERIX, I'M JUST GOING TO ASK ZURIX IF HE'S GOT ANY CHEESE WITHOUT HOLES IN IT.
SHUT UP AND EAT UP, OBELIX!
I DON'T KNOW... WE CAME HERE LOOKING FOR MOUNTAINS AND WE END UP IN A HOLE EATING HOLES!
SHHH!
27B

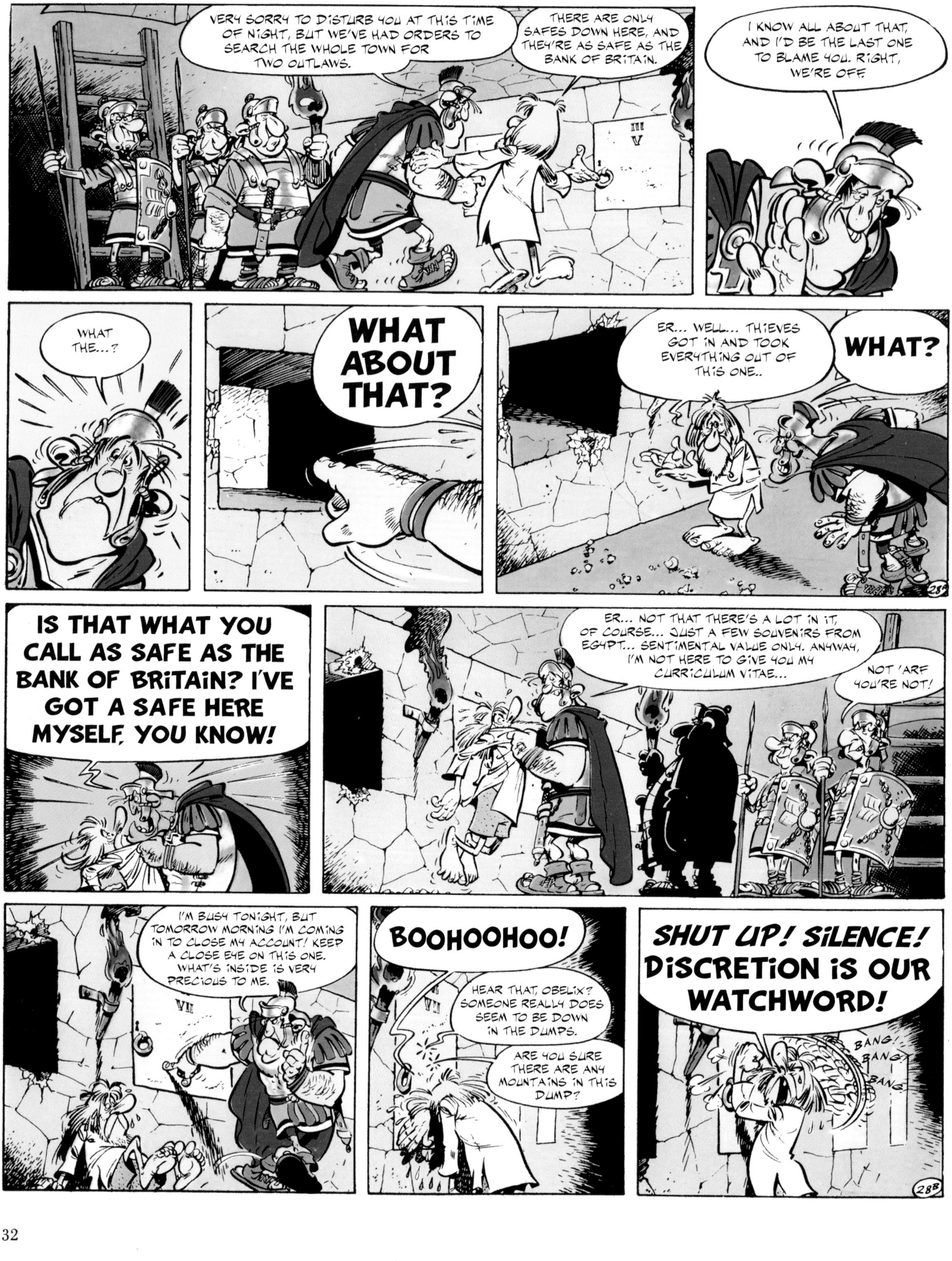
VERY SORRY TO DISTURB YOU AT THIS TIME OF NIGHT, BUT WE'VE HAD ORDERS TO SEARCH THE WHOLE TOWN FOR TWO OUTLAWS.
THERE ARE ONLY SAFES DOWN HERE, AND THEY'RE AS SAFE AS THE BANK OF BRITAIN.
III
V
I KNOW ALL ABOUT THAT, AND I'D BE THE LAST ONE TO BLAME YOU. RIGHT, WE'RE OFF.
WHAT THE...?
WHAT ABOUT THAT?
ER... WELL... THIEVES GOT IN AND TOOK EVERYTHING OUT OF THIS ONE..
WHAT?
IS THAT WHAT YOU CALL AS SAFE AS THE BANK OF BRITAIN? I'VE GOT A SAFE HERE MYSELF, YOU KNOW!
ER... NOT THAT THERE'S A LOT IN IT, OF COURSE... JUST A FEW SOUVENIRS FROM EGYPT... SENTIMENTAL VALUE ONLY. ANYWAY, I'M NOT HERE TO GIVE YOU MY CURRICULUM VITAE...
NOT 'ARF YOU'RE NOT!
I'M BUSY TONIGHT, BUT TOMORROW MORNING I'M COMING IN TO CLOSE MY ACCOUNT! KEEP A CLOSE EYE ON THIS ONE. WHAT'S INSIDE IS VERY PRECIOUS TO ME.
VII
BOOHOOHOO!
HEAR THAT, OBELIX? SOMEONE REALLY DOES SEEM TO BE DOWN IN THE DUMPS.
ARE YOU SURE THERE ARE ANY MOUNTAINS IN THIS DUMP?
SHUT UP! SILENCE! DISCRETION IS OUR WATCHWORD!
BANG!
BANG!
BANG!
288

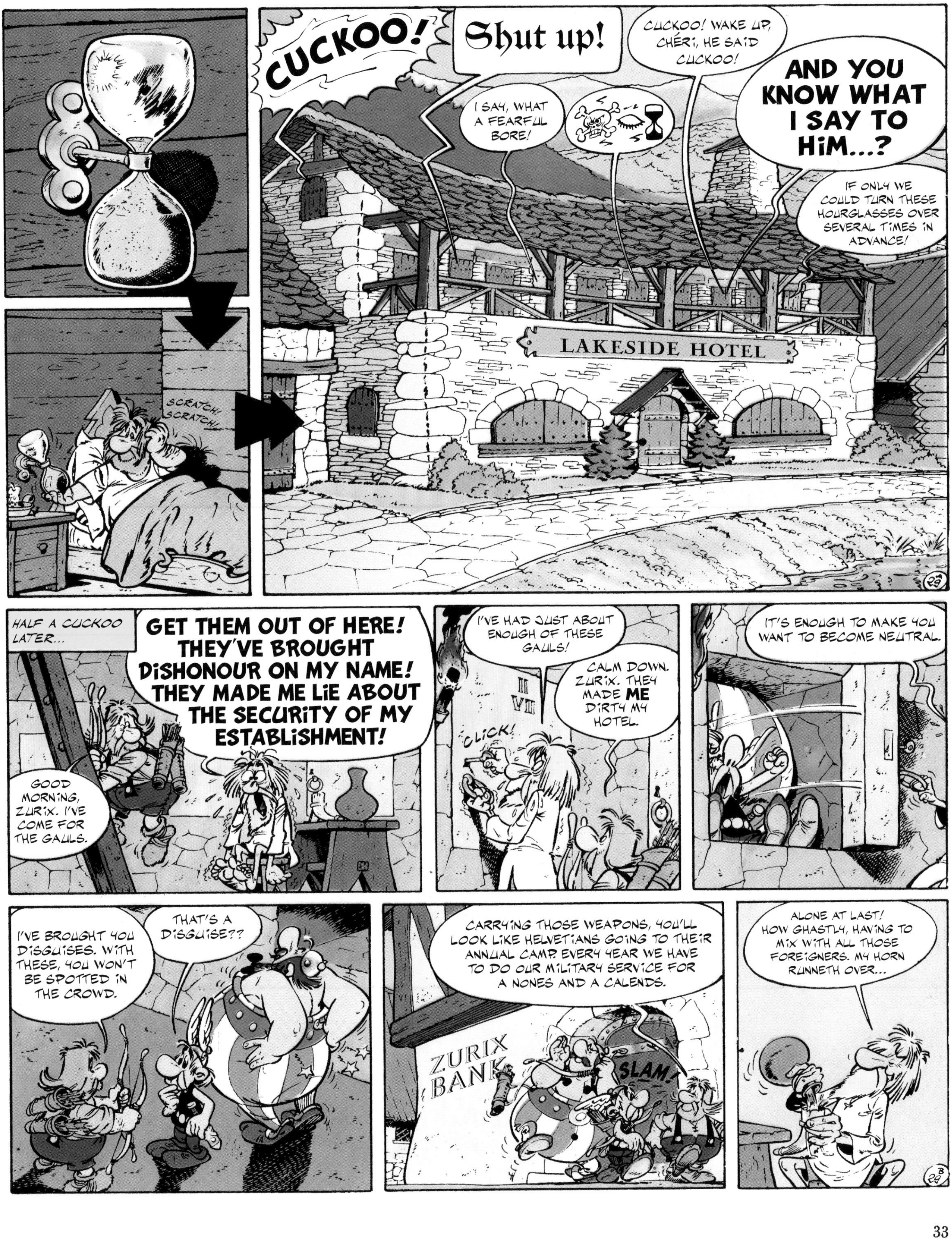
SCRATCH! SCRATCH!
CUCKOO!
Shut up!
I SAY, WHAT A FEARFUL BORE!
CUCKOO! WAKE UP, CHÉRI, HE SAID CUCKOO!
AND YOU KNOW WHAT I SAY TO HIM...?
IF ONLY WE COULD TURN THESE HOURGLASSES OVER SEVERAL TIMES IN ADVANCE!
LAKESIDE HOTEL
HALF A CUCKOO LATER...
GET THEM OUT OF HERE! THEY'VE BROUGHT DISHONOUR ON MY NAME! THEY MADE ME LIE ABOUT THE SECURITY OF MY ESTABLISHMENT!
GOOD MORNING, ZURIX. I'VE COME FOR THE GAULS.
I'VE HAD JUST ABOUT ENOUGH OF THESE GAULS!
CALM DOWN. ZURIX. THEY MADE ME DIRTY MY HOTEL.
CLICK!
IT'S ENOUGH TO MAKE YOU WANT TO BECOME NEUTRAL.
I'VE BROUGHT YOU DISGUISES. WITH THESE, YOU WON'T BE SPOTTED IN THE CROWD.
THAT'S A DISGUISE??
CARRYING THOSE WEAPONS, YOU'LL LOOK LIKE HELVETIANS GOING TO THEIR ANNUAL CAMP. EVERY YEAR WE HAVE TO DO OUR MILITARY SERVICE FOR A NONES AND A CALENDS.
ZURIX BANK
SLAM!
ALONE AT LAST! HOW GHASTLY, HAVING TO MIX WITH ALL THOSE FOREIGNERS. MY HORN RUNNETH OVER...

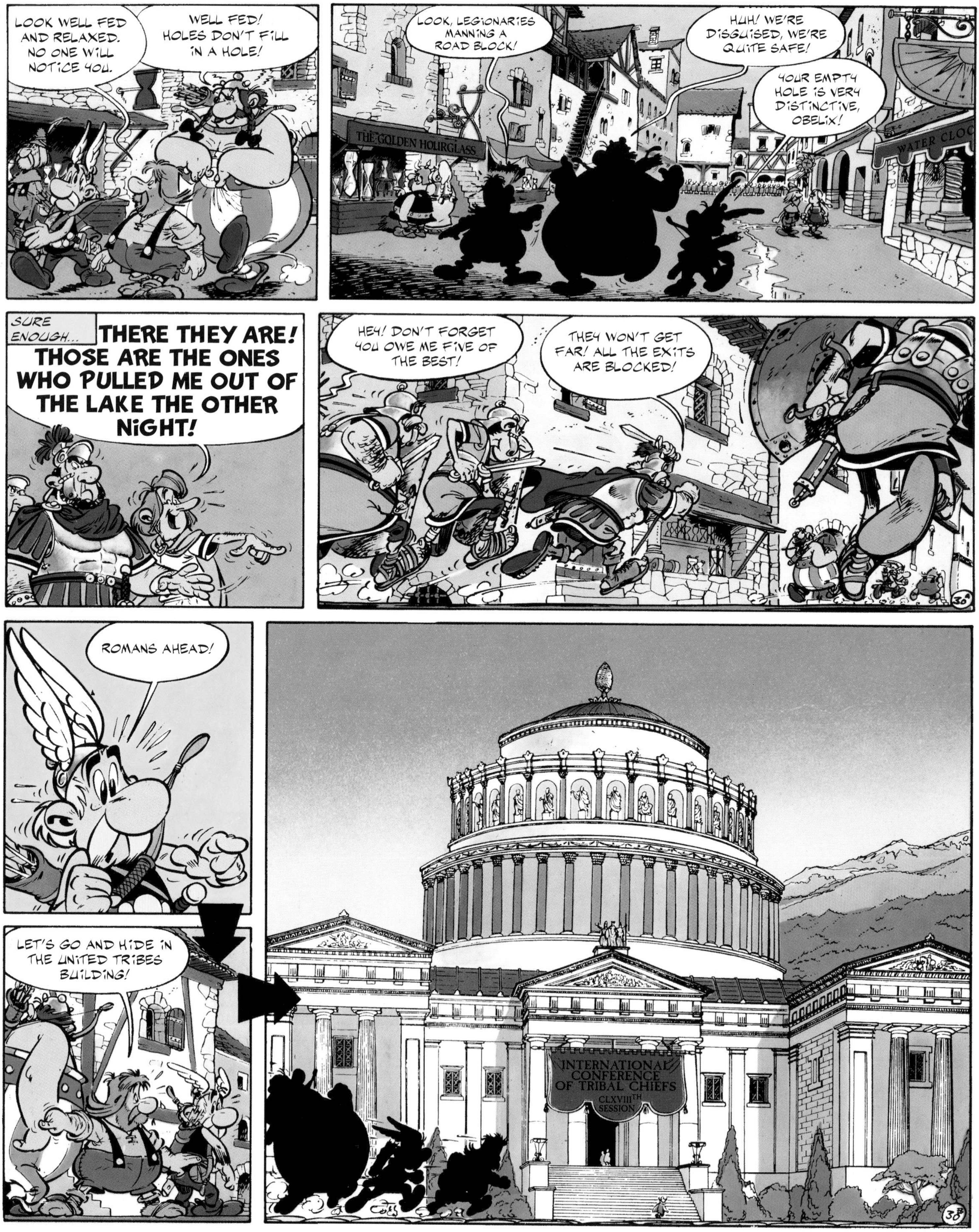
LOOK WELL FED AND RELAXED. NO ONE WILL NOTICE YOU.
WELL FED! HOLES DON'T FILL IN A HOLE!
LOOK, LEGIONARIES MANNING A ROAD BLOCK!
HUH! WE'RE DISGUISED, WE'RE QUITE SAFE!
YOUR EMPTY HOLE IS VERY DISTINCTIVE, OBELIX!
THE GOLDEN HOURGLASS
SURE ENOUGH...
THERE THEY ARE! THOSE ARE THE ONES WHO PULLED ME OUT OF THE LAKE THE OTHER NIGHT!
HEY! DON'T FORGET YOU OWE ME FIVE OF THE BEST!
THEY WON'T GET FAR! ALL THE EXITS ARE BLOCKED!
ROMANS AHEAD!
LET'S GO AND HIDE IN THE UNITED TRIBES BUILDING!
INTERNATIONAL CONFERENCE OF TRIBAL CHIEFS
CLXVIII[TH] SESSION

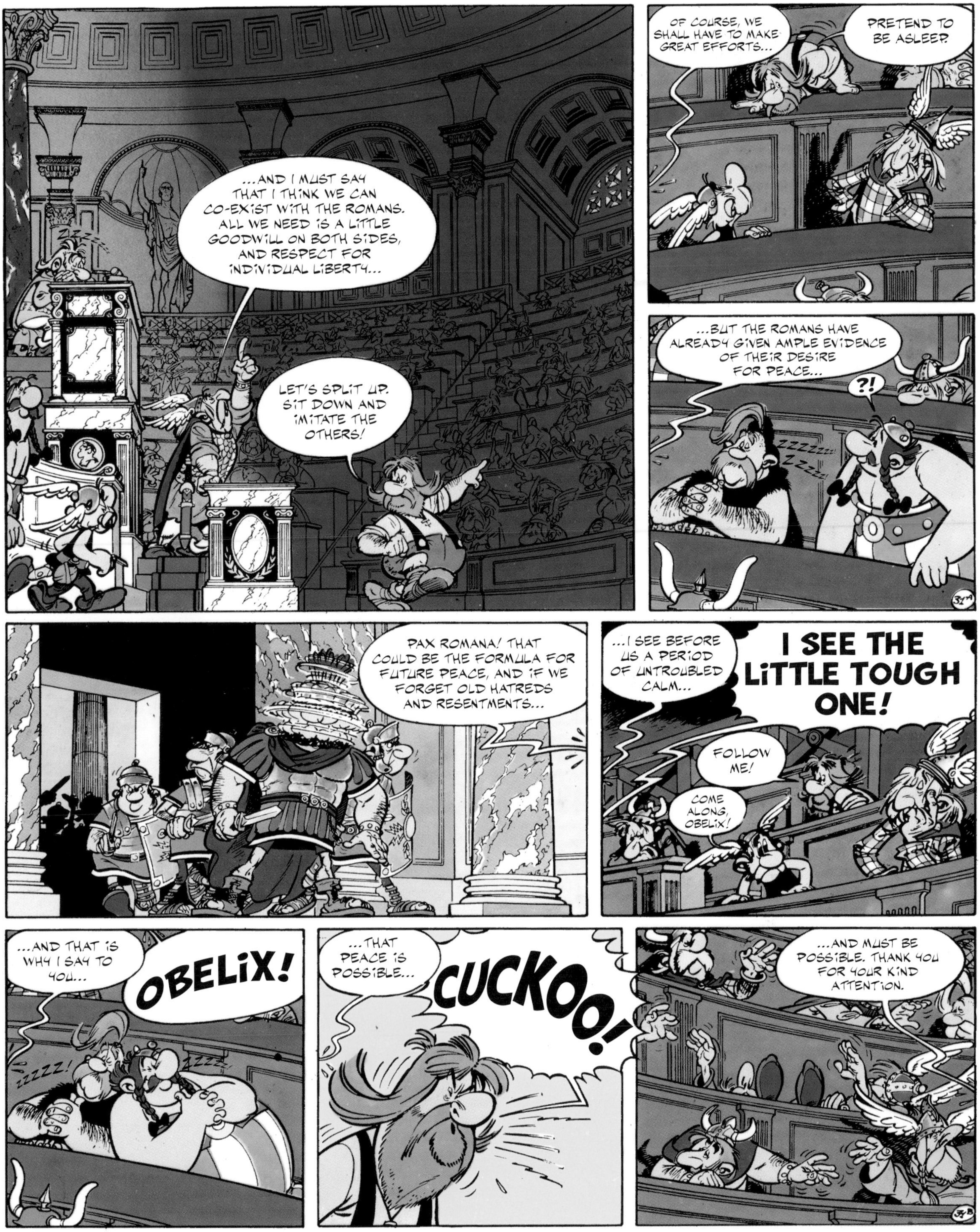
...AND I MUST SAY THAT I THINK WE CAN CO-EXIST WITH THE ROMANS. ALL WE NEED IS A LITTLE GOODWILL ON BOTH SIDES, AND RESPECT FOR INDIVIDUAL LIBERTY...
LET'S SPLIT UP. SIT DOWN AND IMITATE THE OTHERS!
OF COURSE, WE SHALL HAVE TO MAKE GREAT EFFORTS...
PRETEND TO BE ASLEEP?
...BUT THE ROMANS HAVE ALREADY GIVEN AMPLE EVIDENCE OF THEIR DESIRE FOR PEACE...
?!
PAX ROMANA! THAT COULD BE THE FORMULA FOR FUTURE PEACE, AND IF WE FORGET OLD HATREDS AND RESENTMENTS...
...I SEE BEFORE US A PERIOD OF UNTROUBLED CALM...
I SEE THE LITTLE TOUGH ONE!
FOLLOW ME!
COME ALONG, OBELIX!
...AND THAT IS WHY I SAY TO YOU...
OBELIX!
...THAT PEACE IS POSSIBLE...
CUCKOO!
...AND MUST BE POSSIBLE. THANK YOU FOR YOUR KIND ATTENTION.

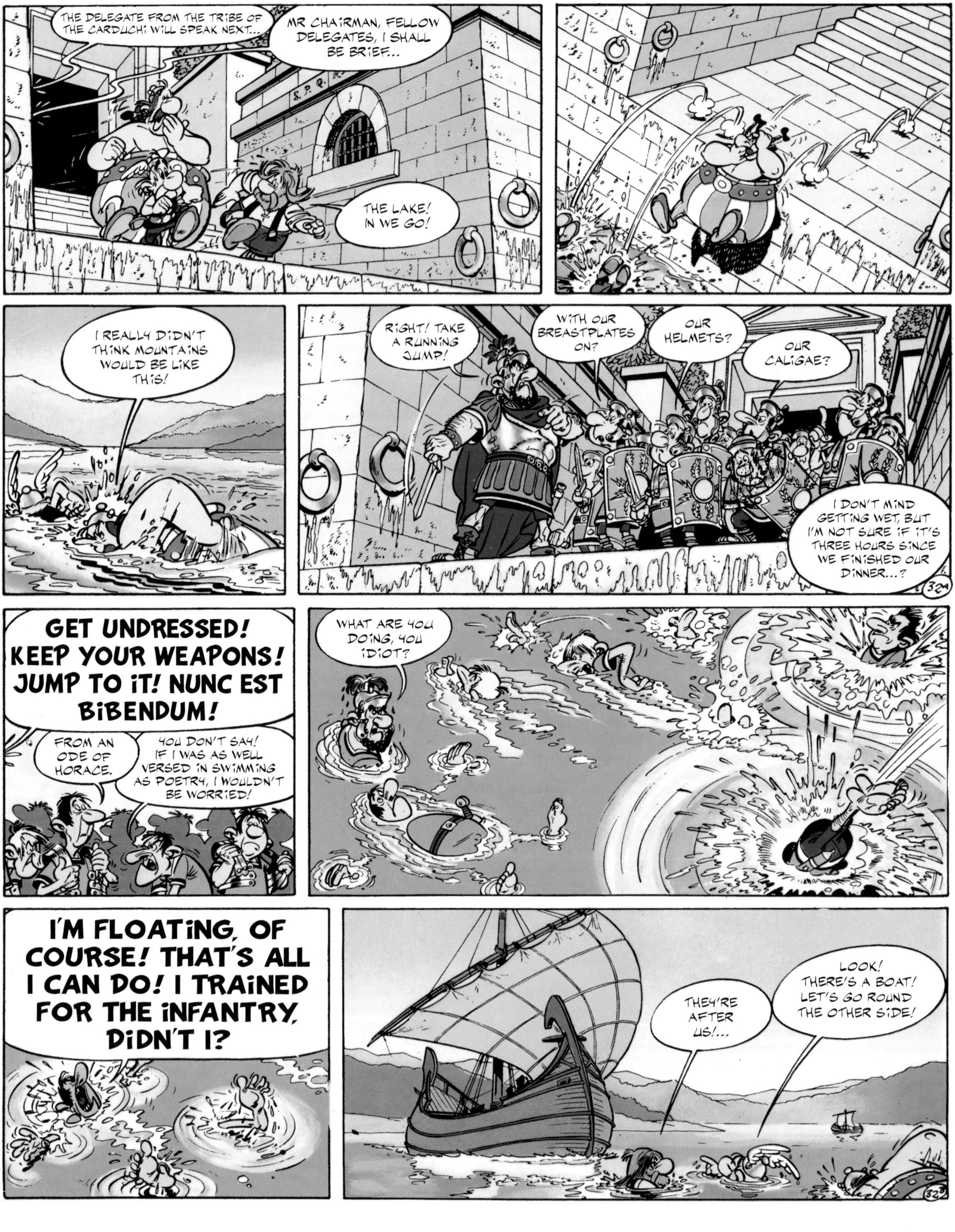
THE DELEGATE FROM THE TRIBE OF THE CARDUCHI WILL SPEAK NEXT...
MR CHAIRMAN, FELLOW DELEGATES, I SHALL BE BRIEF...
THE LAKE! IN WE GO!
I REALLY DIDN'T THINK MOUNTAINS WOULD BE LIKE THIS!
RIGHT! TAKE A RUNNING JUMP!
WITH OUR BREASTPLATES ON?
OUR HELMETS?
OUR CALIGAE?
I DON'T MIND GETTING WET, BUT I'M NOT SURE IF IT'S THREE HOURS SINCE WE FINISHED OUR DINNER...?
GET UNDRESSED! KEEP YOUR WEAPONS! JUMP TO IT! NUNC EST BIBENDUM!
FROM AN ODE OF HORACE.
YOU DON'T SAY! IF I WAS AS WELL VERSED IN SWIMMING AS POETRY, I WOULDN'T BE WORRIED!
WHAT ARE YOU DOING, YOU IDIOT?
I'M FLOATING, OF COURSE! THAT'S ALL I CAN DO! I TRAINED FOR THE INFANTRY, DIDN'T I?
LOOK! THERE'S A BOAT! LET'S GO ROUND THE OTHER SIDE!
THEY'RE AFTER US!...

WHERE'VE THEY GONE? THEY'VE DISAPPEARED!

THEY MUST REALLY BE GETTING INTO DEEP WATER!

FOLLOW THAT BOAT!

HE'S A RIGHT WET, THAT ONE!

YOU'RE OBVIOUSLY NOT FROM ROUND HERE, OR YOU'D KNOW THE BRIDGE CAESAR DESTROYED HAS BEEN REBUILT.

WE KNOW THAT. THANKS FOR THE RESCUE. WE WERE ALL AT SEA IN THERE!

OLELEiiiiiiiiiiiii!
YODLEiOOOOOOOO!

THAT'S A NATIONAL SONG. YOU'RE IN LUCK. YOU CAN HEAR OUR GLEE CLUB.

WE'VE GOT A BARD AT HOME WHO SINGS A BIT LIKE THAT.

OLEiiiiii

OBELIX! COME BACK UP HERE IMMEDIATELY!

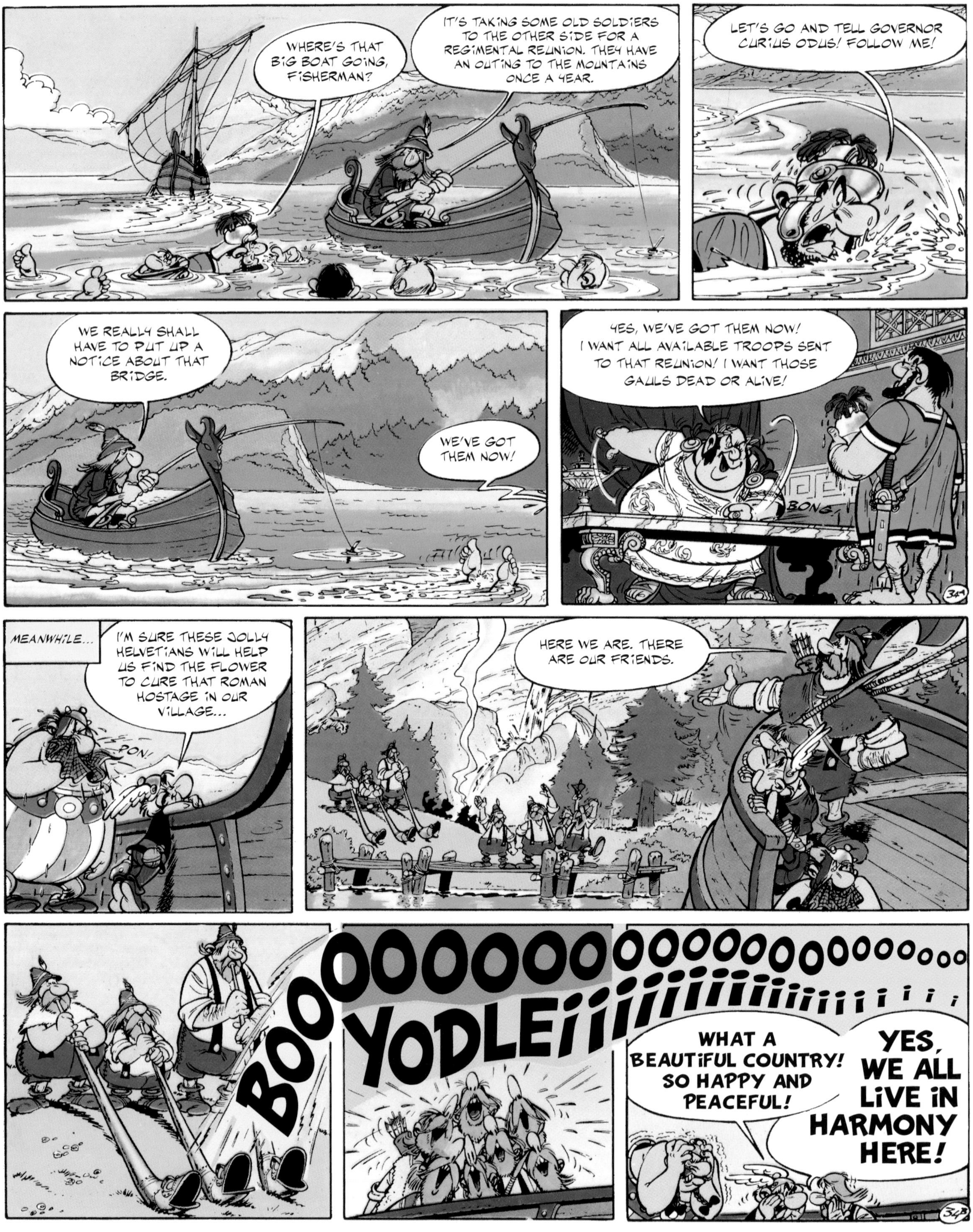

WHERE'S THAT BIG BOAT GOING, FISHERMAN?
IT'S TAKING SOME OLD SOLDIERS TO THE OTHER SIDE FOR A REGIMENTAL REUNION. THEY HAVE AN OUTING TO THE MOUNTAINS ONCE A YEAR.
LET'S GO AND TELL GOVERNOR CURIUS ODUS! FOLLOW ME!
WE REALLY SHALL HAVE TO PUT UP A NOTICE ABOUT THAT BRIDGE.
WE'VE GOT THEM NOW!
YES, WE'VE GOT THEM NOW! I WANT ALL AVAILABLE TROOPS SENT TO THAT REUNION! I WANT THOSE GAULS DEAD OR ALIVE!
BONG
MEANWHILE...
I'M SURE THESE JOLLY HELVETIANS WILL HELP US FIND THE FLOWER TO CURE THAT ROMAN HOSTAGE IN OUR VILLAGE...
PON!
HERE WE ARE. THERE ARE OUR FRIENDS.
BOOOOOOOOOOOOOOOOOOOOOOooo
YODLEiiiiiiiiiiiiiiiiiiiiii
WHAT A BEAUTIFUL COUNTRY! SO HAPPY AND PEACEFUL!
YES, WE ALL LIVE IN HARMONY HERE!

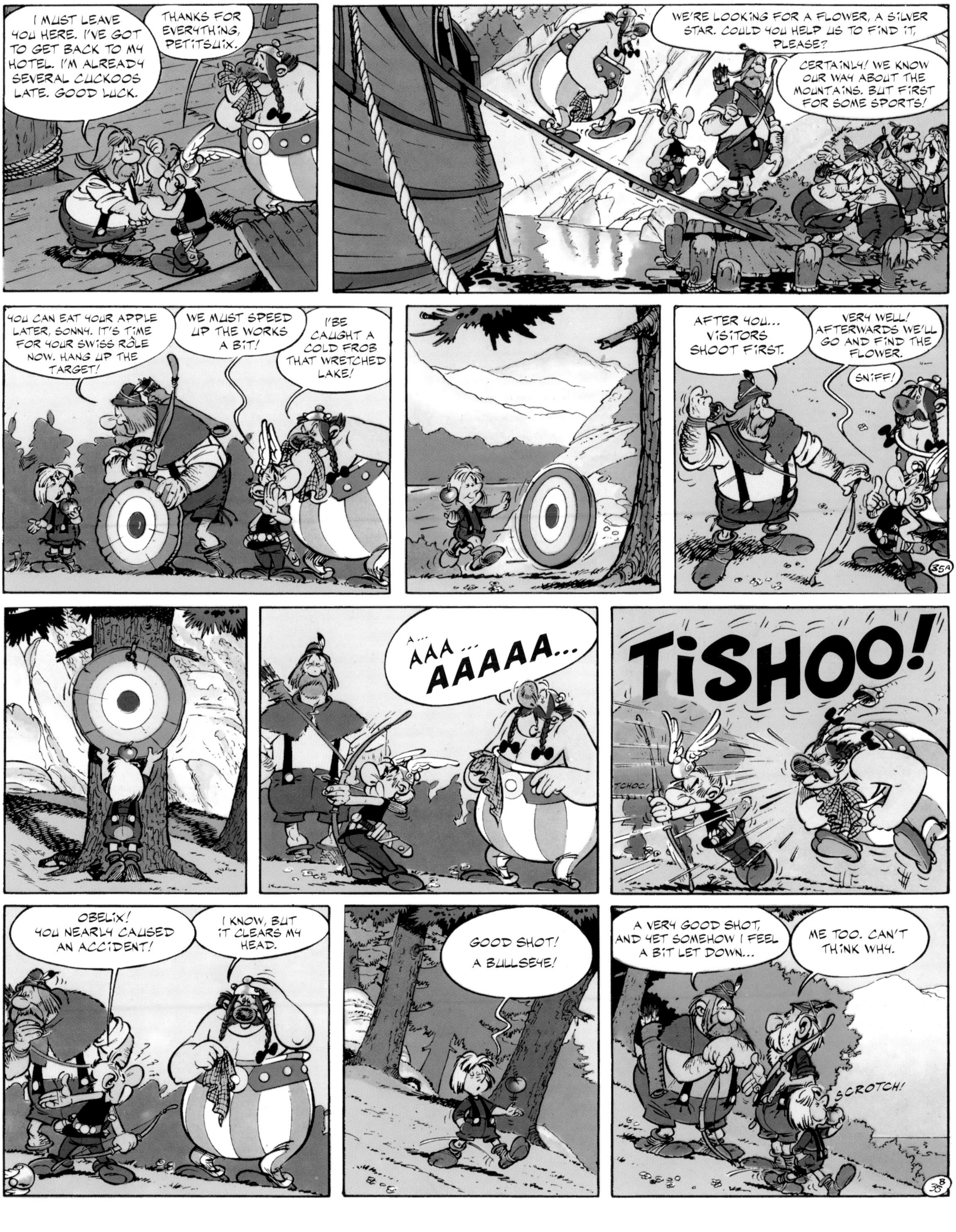
I MUST LEAVE YOU HERE. I'VE GOT TO GET BACK TO MY HOTEL. I'M ALREADY SEVERAL CUCKOOS LATE. GOOD LUCK.
THANKS FOR EVERYTHING, PETITSUIX.
WE'RE LOOKING FOR A FLOWER, A SILVER STAR. COULD YOU HELP US TO FIND IT, PLEASE?
CERTAINLY! WE KNOW OUR WAY ABOUT THE MOUNTAINS. BUT FIRST FOR SOME SPORTS!
YOU CAN EAT YOUR APPLE LATER, SONNY. IT'S TIME FOR YOUR SWISS RÔLE NOW. HANG UP THE TARGET!
WE MUST SPEED UP THE WORKS A BIT!
I'BE CAUGHT A COLD FROB THAT WRETCHED LAKE!
AFTER YOU... VISITORS SHOOT FIRST.
VERY WELL! AFTERWARDS WE'LL GO AND FIND THE FLOWER.
SNIFF!
A... AAA... AAAAA...
TISHOO!
TCHOO!
OBELIX! YOU NEARLY CAUSED AN ACCIDENT!
I KNOW, BUT IT CLEARS MY HEAD.
GOOD SHOT! A BULLSEYE!
A VERY GOOD SHOT, AND YET SOMEHOW I FEEL A BIT LET DOWN...
ME TOO. CAN'T THINK WHY.
SCROTCH!

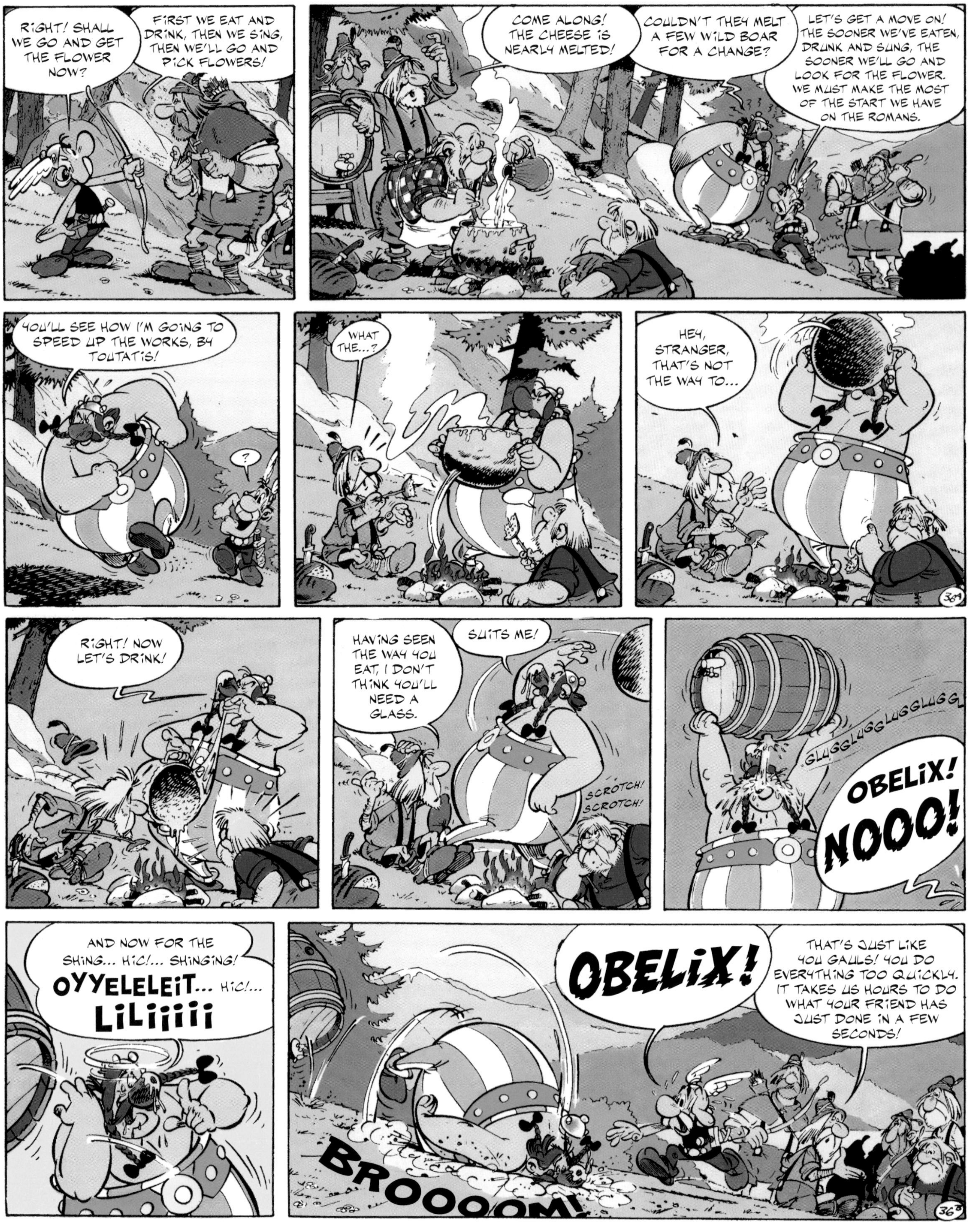

RIGHT! SHALL WE GO AND GET THE FLOWER NOW?
FIRST WE EAT AND DRINK, THEN WE SING, THEN WE'LL GO AND PICK FLOWERS!
COME ALONG! THE CHEESE IS NEARLY MELTED!
COULDN'T THEY MELT A FEW WILD BOAR FOR A CHANGE?
LET'S GET A MOVE ON! THE SOONER WE'VE EATEN, DRUNK AND SUNG, THE SOONER WE'LL GO AND LOOK FOR THE FLOWER. WE MUST MAKE THE MOST OF THE START WE HAVE ON THE ROMANS.
YOU'LL SEE HOW I'M GOING TO SPEED UP THE WORKS, BY TOUTATIS!
?
WHAT THE...?
HEY, STRANGER, THAT'S NOT THE WAY TO...
RIGHT! NOW LET'S DRINK!
HAVING SEEN THE WAY YOU EAT, I DON'T THINK YOU'LL NEED A GLASS.
SUITS ME!
SCROTCH! SCROTCH!
GLUGGLUGGLUGGLUGG
OBELIX! NOOO!
AND NOW FOR THE SHING... HIC!... SHINGING!
OYYELELEIT... HIC!... LILIiiiii
OBELIX!
THAT'S JUST LIKE YOU GAULS! YOU DO EVERYTHING TOO QUICKLY. IT TAKES US HOURS TO DO WHAT YOUR FRIEND HAS JUST DONE IN A FEW SECONDS!
BROOOOOM!

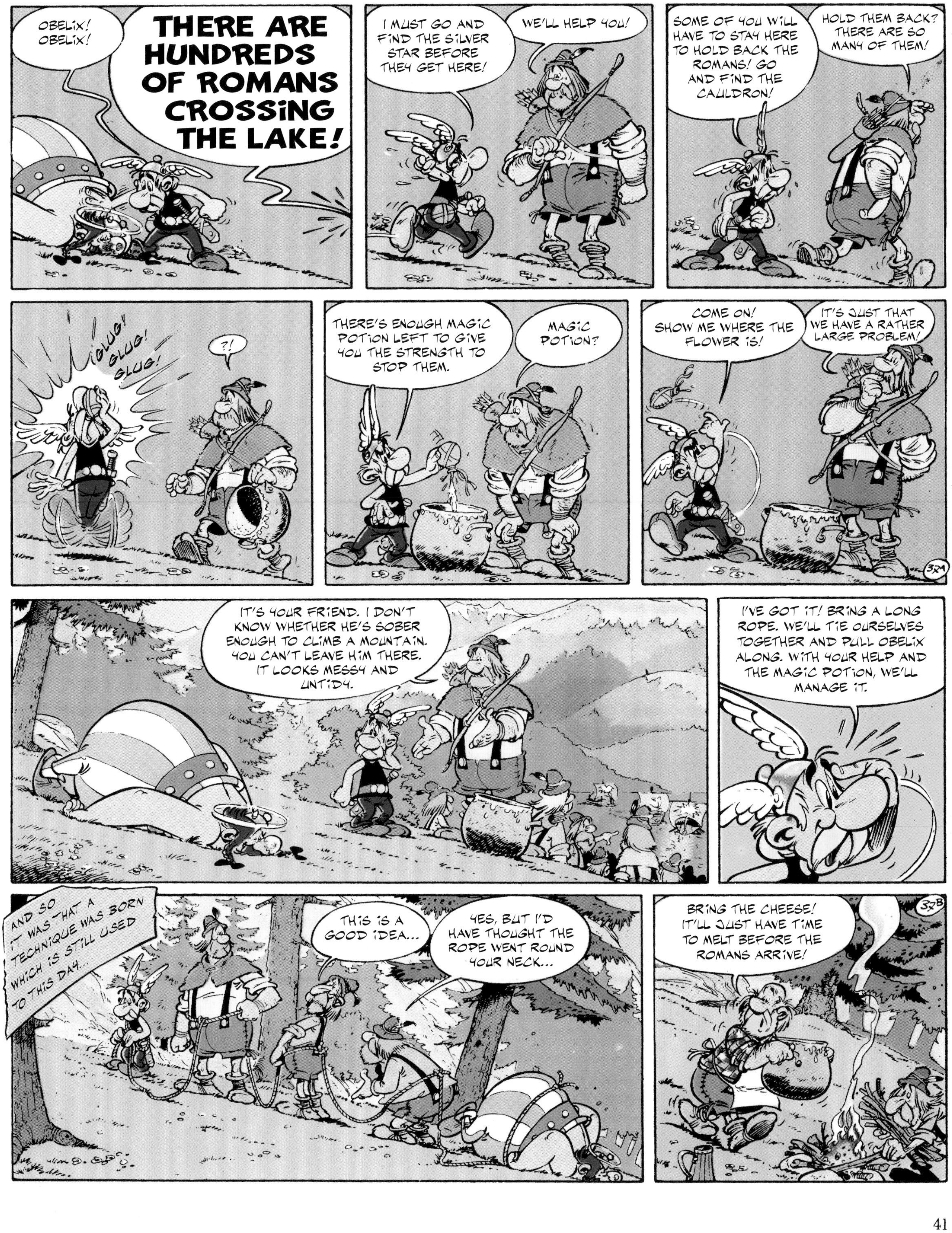

OBELIX! OBELIX!
THERE ARE HUNDREDS OF ROMANS CROSSING THE LAKE!
I MUST GO AND FIND THE SILVER STAR BEFORE THEY GET HERE!
WE'LL HELP YOU!
SOME OF YOU WILL HAVE TO STAY HERE TO HOLD BACK THE ROMANS! GO AND FIND THE CAULDRON!
HOLD THEM BACK? THERE ARE SO MANY OF THEM!
GLUG! GLUG! GLUG!
?!
THERE'S ENOUGH MAGIC POTION LEFT TO GIVE YOU THE STRENGTH TO STOP THEM.
MAGIC POTION?
COME ON! SHOW ME WHERE THE FLOWER IS!
IT'S JUST THAT WE HAVE A RATHER LARGE PROBLEM!
IT'S YOUR FRIEND. I DON'T KNOW WHETHER HE'S SOBER ENOUGH TO CLIMB A MOUNTAIN. YOU CAN'T LEAVE HIM THERE. IT LOOKS MESSY AND UNTIDY.
I'VE GOT IT! BRING A LONG ROPE. WE'LL TIE OURSELVES TOGETHER AND PULL OBELIX ALONG. WITH YOUR HELP AND THE MAGIC POTION, WE'LL MANAGE IT.
AND SO IT WAS THAT A TECHNIQUE WAS BORN WHICH IS STILL USED TO THIS DAY...
THIS IS A GOOD IDEA...
YES, BUT I'D HAVE THOUGHT THE ROPE WENT ROUND YOUR NECK...
BRING THE CHEESE! IT'LL JUST HAVE TIME TO MELT BEFORE THE ROMANS ARRIVE!

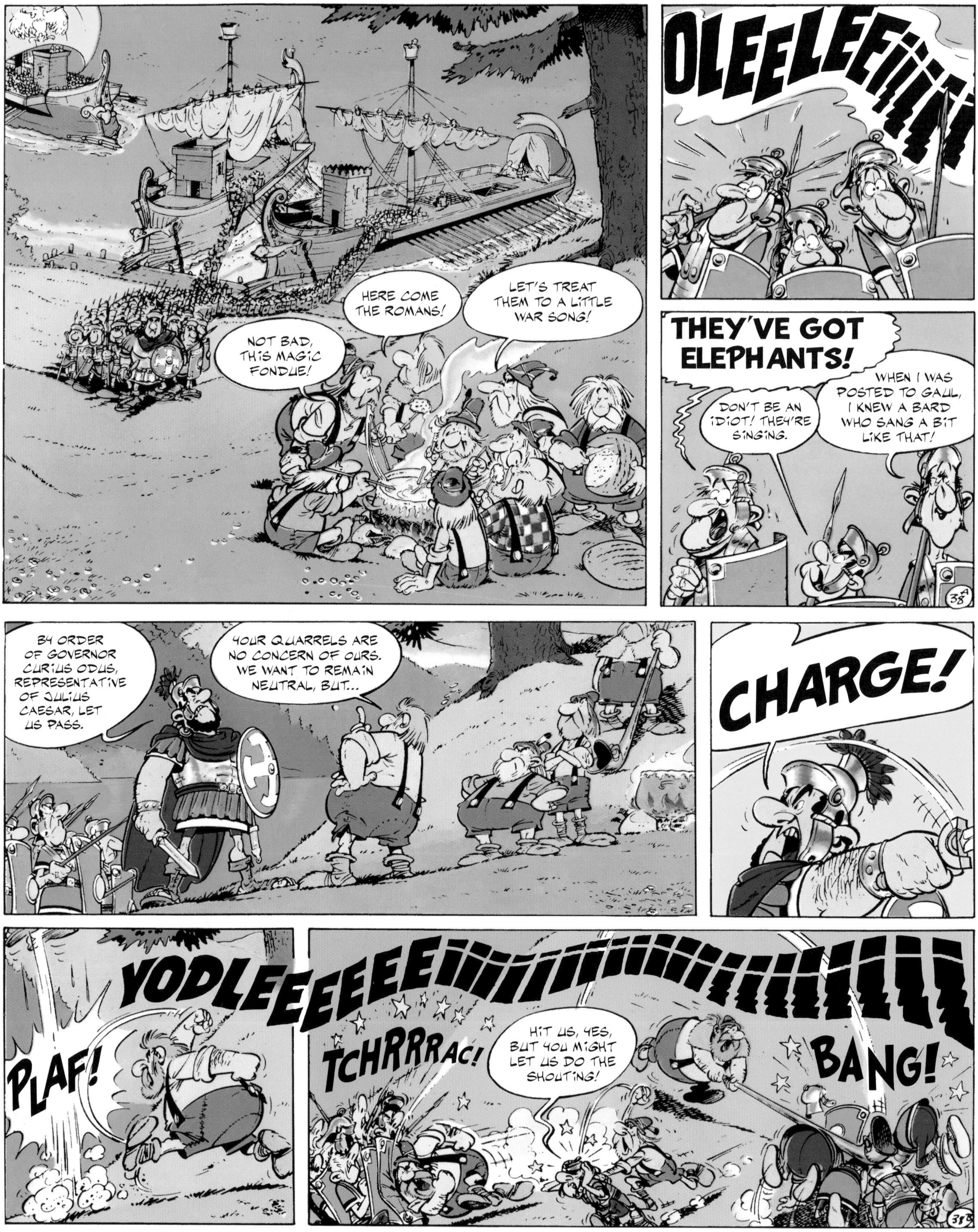

NOT BAD, THIS MAGIC FONDUE!
HERE COME THE ROMANS!
LET'S TREAT THEM TO A LITTLE WAR SONG!
OLEELEEIIIII
THEY'VE GOT ELEPHANTS!
DON'T BE AN IDIOT! THEY'RE SINGING.
WHEN I WAS POSTED TO GAUL, I KNEW A BARD WHO SANG A BIT LIKE THAT!
BY ORDER OF GOVERNOR CURIUS ODUS, REPRESENTATIVE OF JULIUS CAESAR, LET US PASS.
YOUR QUARRELS ARE NO CONCERN OF OURS. WE WANT TO REMAIN NEUTRAL, BUT...
CHARGE!
YODLEEEEEEIIIIIIIIIIIIIIIIIII
PLAF!
TCHRRRAC!
HIT US, YES, BUT YOU MIGHT LET US DO THE SHOUTING!
BANG!

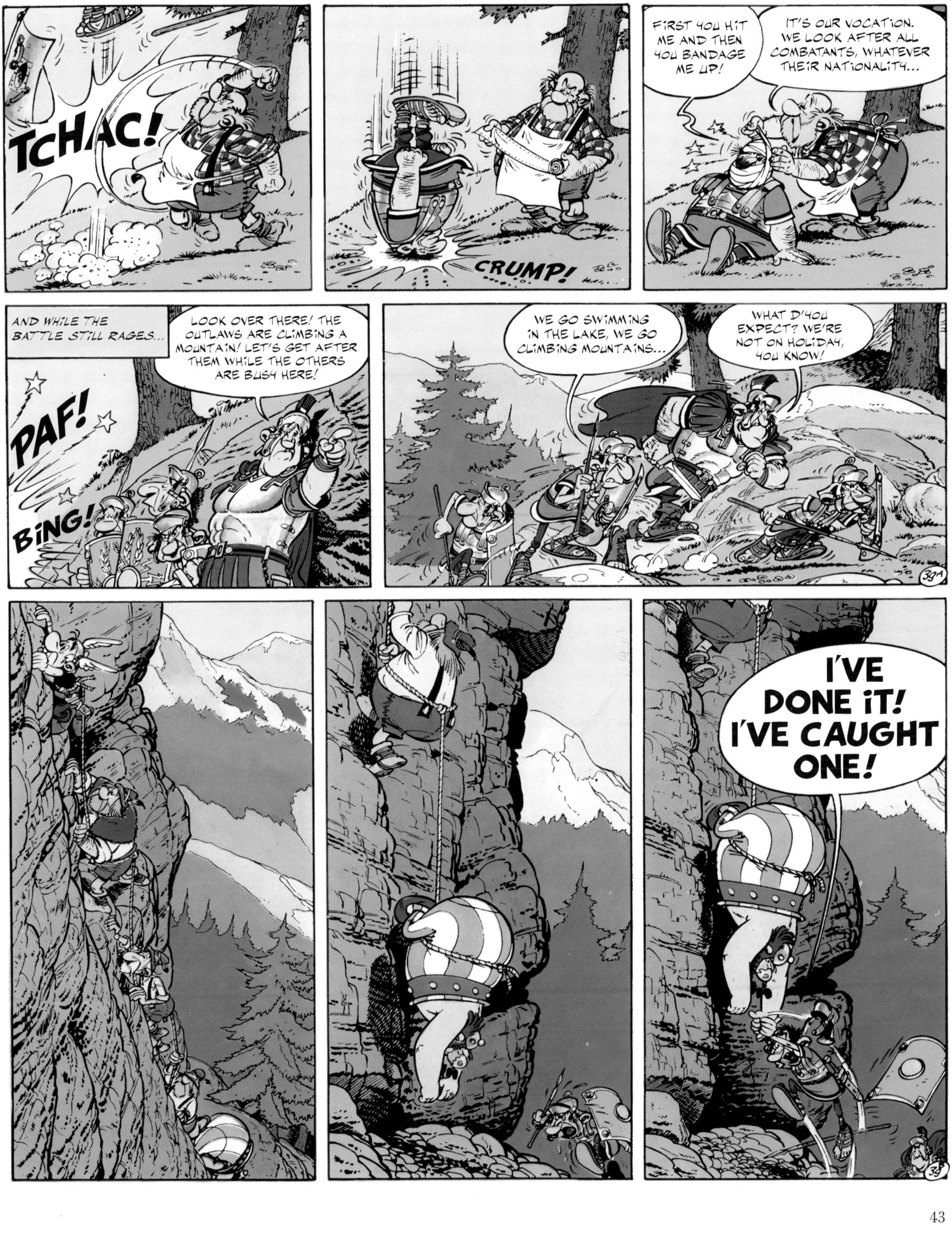
TCHAC!
CRUMP!
FIRST YOU HIT ME AND THEN YOU BANDAGE ME UP!
IT'S OUR VOCATION. WE LOOK AFTER ALL COMBATANTS, WHATEVER THEIR NATIONALITY...
AND WHILE THE BATTLE STILL RAGES...
PAF!
BING!
LOOK OVER THERE! THE OUTLAWS ARE CLIMBING A MOUNTAIN! LET'S GET AFTER THEM WHILE THE OTHERS ARE BUSY HERE!
WE GO SWIMMING IN THE LAKE, WE GO CLIMBING MOUNTAINS...
WHAT D'YOU EXPECT? WE'RE NOT ON HOLIDAY, YOU KNOW!
I'VE DONE IT! I'VE CAUGHT ONE!

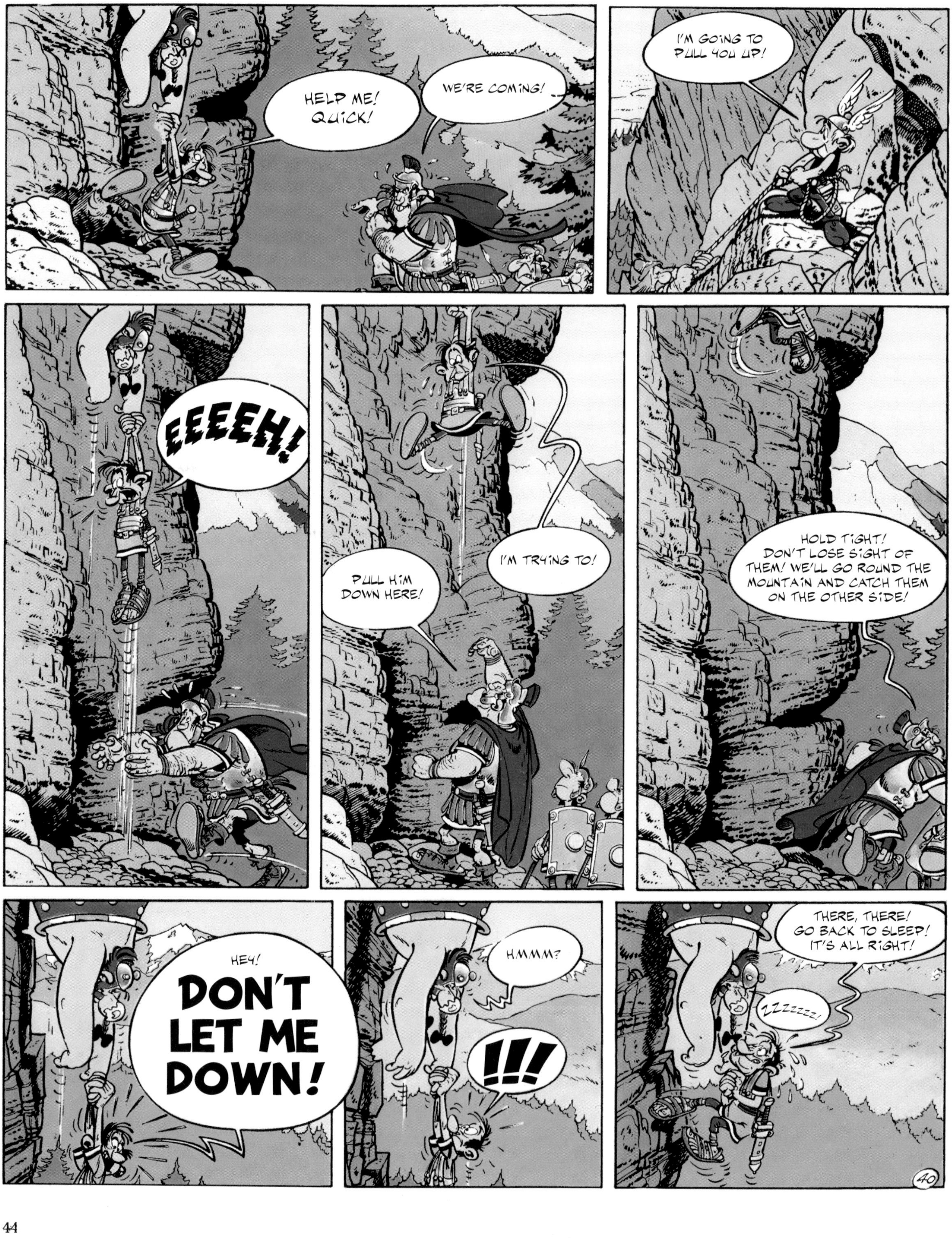
HELP ME! QUICK!
WE'RE COMING!
I'M GOING TO PULL YOU UP!
EEEEH!
PULL HIM DOWN HERE!
I'M TRYING TO!
HOLD TIGHT! DON'T LOSE SIGHT OF THEM! WE'LL GO ROUND THE MOUNTAIN AND CATCH THEM ON THE OTHER SIDE!
HEY! DON'T LET ME DOWN!
HMMM?
!!!
THERE, THERE! GO BACK TO SLEEP! IT'S ALL RIGHT!
ZZZzzzz!
40

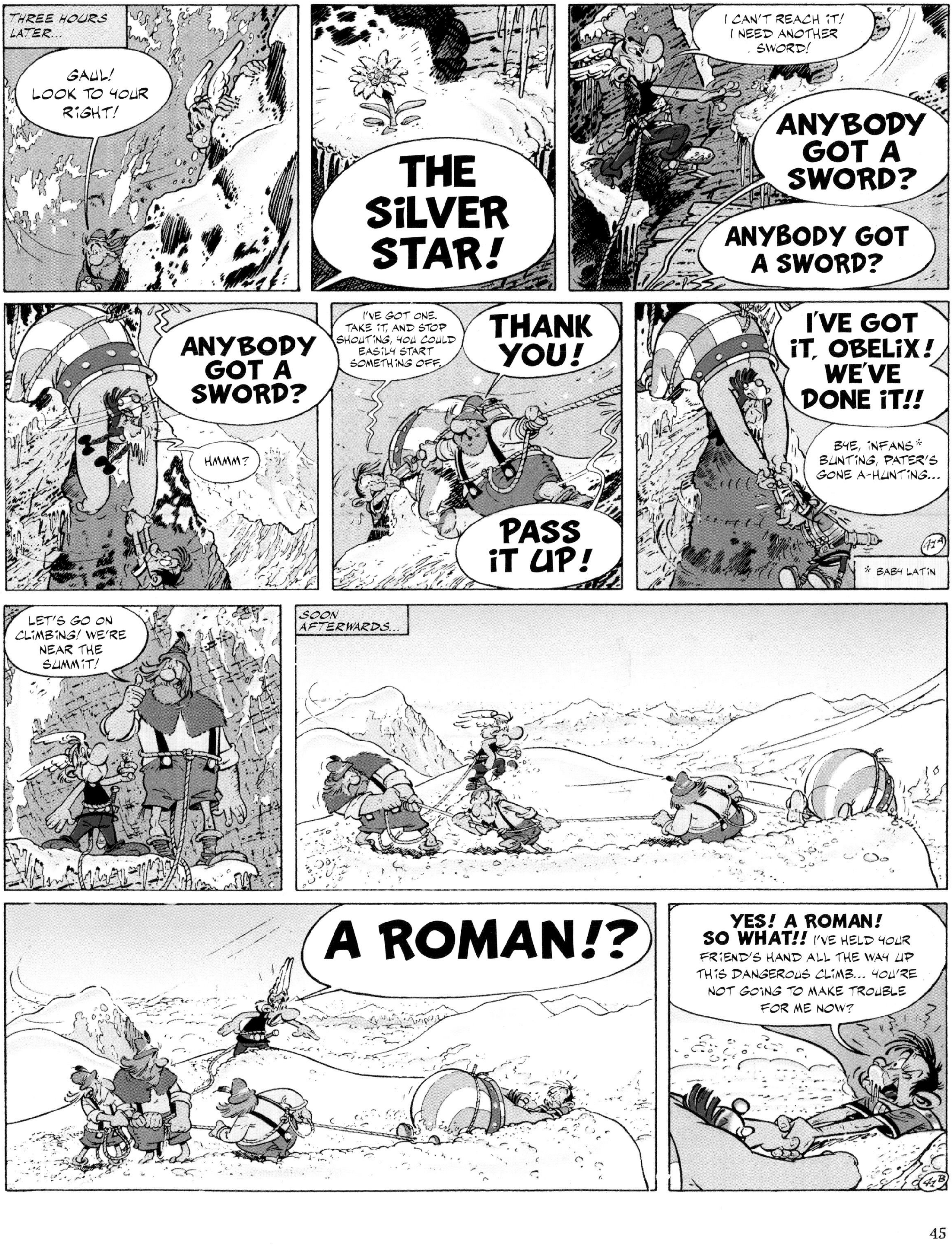
THREE HOURS LATER...
GAUL! LOOK TO YOUR RIGHT!
THE SILVER STAR!
I CAN'T REACH IT! I NEED ANOTHER SWORD!
ANYBODY GOT A SWORD?
ANYBODY GOT A SWORD?
ANYBODY GOT A SWORD?
HMMM?
I'VE GOT ONE. TAKE IT, AND STOP SHOUTING, YOU COULD EASILY START SOMETHING OFF.
THANK YOU!
PASS IT UP!
I'VE GOT IT, OBELIX! WE'VE DONE IT!!
BYE, INFANS* BUNTING, PATER'S GONE A-HUNTING...
* BABY LATIN
LET'S GO ON CLIMBING! WE'RE NEAR THE SUMMIT!
SOON AFTERWARDS...
A ROMAN!?
YES! A ROMAN! SO WHAT!! I'VE HELD YOUR FRIEND'S HAND ALL THE WAY UP THIS DANGEROUS CLIMB... YOU'RE NOT GOING TO MAKE TROUBLE FOR ME NOW?